Brand of the Star

BRAND OF THE STAR

T.V. OLSEN

THORNDIKE
CHIVERS

This Large Print edition is published by Thorndike Press, Waterville, Maine, USA and by AudioGO Ltd, Bath, England.

Thorndike Press, a part of Gale, Cengage Learning.

The text of this Large Print edition is unabridged.
Other aspects of the book may vary from the original edition.
Set in 16 pt. Plantin.

LIBRARY OF CONGRESS CATALOGING-IN-PUBLICATION DATA

Olsen, Theodore V.
  Brand of the star / by T.V. Olsen.
    p. cm. — (Thorndike Press large print western)
  ISBN-13: 978-1-4104-3589-7
  ISBN-10: 1-4104-3589-X
  1. Large type books. I. Title.
PS3565.L8B73 2011
813'.54—dc22   2010050265

BRITISH LIBRARY CATALOGUING-IN-PUBLICATION DATA AVAILABLE

Published in 2011 in the U.S. by arrangement with Golden West Literary Agency.
Published in 2011 in the U.K. by arrangement with Golden West Literary Agency.

U.K. Hardcover: 978 1 445 83694 2 (Chivers Large Print)
U.K. Softcover: 978 1 445 83695 9 (Camden Large Print)

Printed in the United States of America
1 2 3 4 5 6 7 15 14 13 12 11

BRAND OF THE STAR

CHAPTER ONE

As true dawn straddled the hill-brushing horizon with its first belts of rosegold, Sam Ashby crested a steep rise and halted his bay mare. His gaze swept the flats below, their dun monotony broken only by the meandering flow of Tie Creek, now roiling deep with meltwater from the spring thaw. In a sense, that barren sweep was the key to this vast, trough-shaped basin. For this was the central trunk of the creek which, toward the south, split into many branches, spreading verdancy to the rich soils of the lower basin. A fitting place for the rendezvous, this stream which divides the basin, ran Sam's brief thought with no irony in it, because his was a hard-bitten and practical nature with little space for frivolity.

But a fine edge of impatience lay against Sam Ashby's thoughts as he studied the terrain. He was a towering man of thirty-two, gaunted to bone and lean muscle, who sat his saddle with the easy slouch of a lifetime horseman. His weathered face was long and bony, its sharp lines and cold gray eyes lending a cast of sober alertness; his straight mouth with its down-tucked corners, strengthening his looks, stamped him as a man whose humor was rarely shown, and then only in dry and biting fashion. His hair was straight and black as an Indian's; his battered, sweat-stained Stetson rode atop it without crease or flourish. His heavy trousers were stuffed into full-length cowman's boots. A threadbare black vest spanned by a brass watch chain was buttoned over his flannel shirt.

Sam reached for the watch. Yes . . . he was on time, and where the hell was Paddy — and the others?

He gigged his mare down the slope, his frown not easing until, as he neared its base, he saw the tan dust of an approaching rider from the southeast. Shortly, two others rounded a swatch of hills from the north. All converged on the first creek forking toward the north edge of the flats, and Sam was the first to arrive. Boone MacLaughlin was next, replying to Sam's greeting with the barest nod.

MacLaughlin was big-boned and lean-shanked, with a gaunt Lincolnesque face under a crisp saddle of sandy hair. Still in his mid-twenties, he was slightly stooped with hard work. His intense reserve bordered on surliness, a trait for which Sam, himself taciturn, did not censure him. Moreover, MacLaughlin had good reason for the venomous bitterness that lay like a banked fire in his pale eyes.

They sat their horses wordlessly, waiting for the other two. Within five minutes, Chet Bannerman, coming at an impetuous pace, ironhanded his slobbering mount to a stop and pranced it sideways a few show-off steps. Boone MacLaughlin's brooding stare held open anger; Sam concealed his own disgust beneath an impassive nod.

"How are you, Ashby?" Chet said loudly, giving Boone only an amused, contemptuous glance. Chet Bannerman was thin as a rail, gawky as an adolescent. Actually he had lived twenty-two years but had not a lick of sense to account for one of them. Despite this, he carried himself with a certain rakish grace heightened by a handsome ax-blade of a face with cat-quick green eyes. He wore a freshly blocked gray Stetson and a fancy *charro* jacket.

"Middlin'," Sam said in a neutral tone. "How's the General?"

At mention of his father, young Bannerman shrugged without interest and looked restlessly away. General Lucius Bannerman was an ex-military careerist whose great ranch, Spanish Spade, covered the entire eastern half of the lower basin. He was an austere man of precise manners, hard to know and harder to understand, but Sam Ashby knew quiet admiration for his industry and hard business head . . . though the Bannerman blood had run water-thin in the General's only son.

Chet's companion now moved up at a restrained trot. This was Milo Squires, foreman of Spanish Spade. He was of an age with Sam, a full head shorter, but long-armed and of a thickset, powerful build. Squires' hair and eyebrows were paler than his dark skin; his face was broad and square, with a wide mouth fixed by a perpetual half-smile. His upper eyelids were hooded by folds of flesh at the outer corners, giving him a sly and sleepy look. Actually he missed little, as his quiet competence revealed.

Like his boss, Milo Squires was an enigma, though a wholly different kind. General Bannerman's aloofness was understandable, bred of a society alien to this blunt land. Squires, who wore his soiled range clothes like a second hide, was baffling in his own

10

right. Sam's feeling for the man bordered on cold dislike, which irritated his practical nature for it was unreasoning, without basis.

Squires gave Boone MacLaughlin a civil nod, said mildly, "How, Sam."

"Milo."

"What's keeping Delaney?"

Sam squinted down the central fork of Tie Creek, which cut through the hills to the town of Elkhorn ten miles away. "Rider coming. That should be Paddy."

Chet Bannerman's chuckle was humorless and a little ugly. "Five men to drive one spic back to his chili patch. By God, they'll be laughing in Mextown tonight."

"Four men and you," Boone MacLaughlin observed surlily. "That ought to really break 'em up."

A swift, pale rage twisted young Bannerman's face. "You dirty pup of a goddamn sheepherder — !"

Both of them reined hard together, and Sam quartered his mare between them at the last moment. His cold stare locked Chet's and held, and the youth sullenly lowered the quirt thronged to his right wrist. Ashby's tone curled around his words like a whiplash:

"Five men. And there'd be five more if the damned fools had listened to me. And if there was a hundred spreads in this basin, I'd have asked for a man from each!"

Milo Squires nodded. "That's right. We got to show the Mex how the vote runs."

"Any 'steader, Mex or not," Sam corrected flatly.

"Sure," Milo said agreeably. "Sore thing."

They sat their mounts then in a weighted silence, watching the coming rider. They were an ill-assorted company, Sam thought wearily, bound only by a brief common purpose, and he would be glad to see it over and done with. . . .

The federal government had laid the ground for what Sam Ashby regarded as a monument to politicking stupidity. The homestead movement had caught on firmly a generation ago, but so far as government records were concerned, Two Troughs Basin had been a part of the big Ute reservation to the north. The first basin settlers had run the Indians off or bargained with them for the land here, then had marked off their own boundary lines. Others, a few late-comers, had bought into those early jackleg claims, but for more than two decades the girdling arm of the Elk Mountains had insulated the basin from any large-scale invasion of settlers. But now the railroad had run in a spur line at the same time that a government surveyor had recommended to the U.S. Land Office that the basin he declared public domain and thrown open to homesteading.

The ranchers had at first been grateful for the laying in of steel, doing away with the necessity of shedding tallow and value from their beeves with long market drives. They'd been, Sam thought wryly, too dumb to see the hitch; those same rails would encourage an influx of hoemen. Yet even federal blessing of the basin as public domain hadn't raised their blood pressures above a notch. After all, the northern half of Two Troughs Basin was unsettled and neglected . . . plenty of room for sodders there. For which there was good reason; the north basin was too high to be benefited by the mountain watershed which released its torrents into the southerly lowlands.

For a time the ranchers' arrogant self-assurance had been justified; the few 'steaders who'd timidly staked out in the clay and sand hills to the north, avoiding the rich, ranch-settled graze below, were shortly driven out by drought and crop failure. When at last one invaded a specific cattleman's territory, it came as a rude shock — for the invader came out of a little Mexican settlement south of Elkhorn. Ordinarily the

13

Mexes tilled their little bean patches, lazed through a happy-go-lucky existence of ten thousand mananas, and kept to themselves except when an outsider came hell-snorting after their women; then slumbering tempers flared in hot blood and sometimes cold steel. But a Mex didn't come hunting trouble.

So the white community was at first more bewildered than angry when young Vicente Gutierrez moved boldly onto Spanish Spade's vast acreage and even had the gall to appropriate a deserted lineshack there, rather than build for himself. Folks tended to put this to Mexicans' natural sloth rather than defiance — though as Sheriff Whit McKeogh, the local philosopher, had acidly observed, the same trait in a white man would be called shrewd economizing. But dammit, men argued, Gutierrez wasn't even American; where did he get off filing a U.S. homestead? Cooler heads opined that since Gutierrez had been born after the Mex territorial cession, he was sure-to-hell a natural citizen. Well, yes, but by God, the Mexes were mostly Injun, and weren't the goddam Injuns all government wards?

Sam Ashby had scant patience for these arguments; he was concerned only with the long-time effect of Gutierrez' bold claim on the south basin's open range. The basin ranchers had already petitioned Washington for recognition of their original unofficial claims. Senators and lawyers were preparing briefs on their behalf. But the seat of government was distant from this isolated basin, cold to its warming passions, and matters were moving slowly. One successful toehold would embolden a flood of entrymen here. Cut it clean at the beginning, Sam declared; stop it cold with a concerted show of hardcore opinion.

But Sam's effort to rally the small ranchers met with a stolid wall of indifference. They were backwoods individualists who handled their own troubles; bedamned if they were going to step on behalf of big, powerful Spanish Spade, for whom none held affection. The greaser was General Bannerman's problem; let old Spit'n'polish shoot his own skunks.

Sam had been surprised when Boone MacLaughlin agreed to come along, representing his own one-loop outfit; this sullen and solitary youth had been a last resort, and from him Sam had least expected a positive response. Next Sam had ridden to Spanish Spade, where General Bannerman had heard him out with cold courtesy and agreed that Sam's position showed sense and foresight. He would send his son and his foreman to rep for Spanish Spade. Sam had also argued Paddy Delaney, deputy sheriff, into joining the party.

Now, as Paddy reined in beside the others, Sam said impatiently, "If you're all ready, let's get to it."

Paddy Delaney took off his hat and sleeved his perspiring brow, a red-haired, youngish man inclined to stoutness, whose round, ever-worried face looked unhappier than usual.

"Hadn't we better be havin' some kind of a plan, Sam? That lineshack is surrounded by open flats. He'll pick up a body of riders in short order — and a hot-headed kid like that, he'll likely start shooting. That's what I'm along to help avoid — or so you said."

"I was coming to that," Sam said, a shade irritably. "Milo, you and Chet ride up to the shack openly. There's a dry wash runs along back of the outbuildings. Rest of us'll circle wide, come up through the wash. While you hold Gutierrez' attention, we'll take him by surprise. . . ."

Sided by Delaney and Boone MacLaughlin, Sam spurred northwest behind a low range of hills. Presently the three descended into a grassy dip where an ancient gully wore a tortuous path into the long flatland

16

beyond. Riding between its steep banks, they would not be spotted. As they rode single file down the gully, Sam taking the lead, Paddy said suddenly:

"Sam, why you really wantin' me on this fandango?"

"Told you before. I want to take Guiterrez without a fight. If anyone feels mean — one of us, or Gutierrez — a lawman overseeing the business should cool trouble before it starts."

"That — maybe. But you've a shrewd head, me lad; and it's in my mind that you hope my presence'll add an air of lawful sanction to the proceeding — and leave your Gutierrez with the mistaken impression that the law stands against him. By heaven, it's with him I should be standing!"

Sam shrugged. "You'll be standing with no one, Paddy. You're along for the reason I said. If someone wants to prove up a homestead, he's got to live on it. We're just seeing Gutierrez doesn't get that chance. You're county law; a federal homestead is no mix of yours. If Gutierrez wants, he can complain to Washington, or the local land office."

"And what will a Mexican's word carry?"

"Look," Sam said sharply, "his being a Mexican has nothing to do with it! Damn it, Paddy; you're a cowman — or your father was. We didn't tame the country to see it broken in farmsteads. This land can't be cropped on large scale; the soil's not much except for forage crops —"

"Aye, the land will break them of itself. Let the sodders learn of it themselves, then."

Sam snorted. "And wreck the country doing it. We sweated blood to make this country, and not for any nester riffraff to grab off. It wasn't them fought Indians or built Elkhorn or tamed down the land. . . . You know me better than that, Paddy."

Delaney sighed. "A man's best friend surely should."

They rode in silence for a while, then Paddy said curiously: "What about Nancy?"

"What about her?"

"She's your wife; what'll she be thinkin' of this business?"

Sam shrugged. "She doesn't like it."

"Truth to tell," Paddy grumbled dryly, "she's not alone. . . ."

A smile flicked the corners of Sam's straight mouth. Good old Paddy . . . with his own brand of stolid courage, yet ever restrained by caution. Still, Paddy had probably hit the mark squarely when he'd said that Sam's insistence on his presence was for less-than-lofty motives. A lot of the high-

18

sounding reasons a man gave himself for a given action were tawdry excuses for some private spite or fear or selfish passion. Boone MacLaughlin, for example . . . Mac-Laughlin, a despised ex-convict, might actually be seizing an opportunity to slap down someone even lower in the human pecking order — a Mexican.

Sam roused from his brooding then, for they had penetrated the flats for a mile, and now he glimpsed the weathered roofs of the old Spanish Spade linecamp. He halted his animal and dismounted, throwing the reins. Paddy and MacLaughlin followed suit, and the three men moved on foot up the dry streambed, next ascending the bank of the wash where it sloped steeply up at the rear of the buildings.

Cautioning the others to silence, Sam moved at a crouching trot along the flank of the makeshift brush corral. A speckle-rumped Appaloosa confined inside pricked up his ears and sidled nervously away. Sam slowed pace, waiting for the beast to make a betraying whicker, and when it did not, he moved on to the shelter of a tool shed, his companions shuffling in his lead.

Sam removed his hat and edged an eye around the shed corner. Across the open yard beyond lay the main shack. He'd hoped they might catch Gutierrez abed . . . but smoke wreathed from the tin roofstack, the smell of fresh coffee wafted across the cool morning air. Now Sam picked up the approach of horsemen from across the flats. If Gutierrez chanced to be near a rear window, the riders' approach would pull him to the front, so now was the time to move. Milo and Chet would draw the Mexican from the shack while the others safely took him from behind.

Motioning Delaney and MacLaughlin to move up on the right flank of the house, Sam slipped his gun from its holster. He ran silently across the open compound, along the left shack wall, ducked low as he passed the single window and halted at the front corner. He saw Milo and Chet coming on at a brisk pace, and he waited, the cedar stock-plates of his old Remington dragoon sweat-slick against his palm.

A dozen yards from the shack, Milo Squires cantered his mount to a sliding halt, lifting his voice. "Hello, the house!"

"What you gringos want?" Gutierrez was ready; he laid down a flat, sharp response from within the open doorway.

"To hand you your walking papers, sonny," Milo taunted. "Come out and get 'em."

At once Gutierrez stepped through the doorway. He held a rifle raised nearly eye-level, pointed at Milo's broad chest.

When Gutierrez was ten feet from the house, Sam stepped out, saying quietly, "There's three guns on your back, son," and added sharply, "Don't do that!" Gutierrez had started to pivot on a heel, halted dead and only stood now, breathing hard.

Paddy and Boone MacLaughlin stepped out from the opposite corner, their pistols leveled. Sam walked to Gutierrez and lifted the rifle from his slack grasp. The youth slanted a glance, bold and black and hating, full on him. "Brave gringos," he jeered. "All five."

Sam had not met Vicente Gutierrez, and he sized the boy up curiously. He was of middle height, slender but with a hint of lithe and wiry strength. His face was pale brown, thin and sensitive, with sharply handsome features; these reflected a quick temper which was usually thinly bridled, Sam guessed, beneath a sullen reserve. This was no manana Mex who happily shed an Americano's arrogant slights; young Gutier-rez carried himself with board-straight pride. He was bareheaded with black hair wild and unruly, and he wore threadbare jeans and a frayed cotton shirt of faded rose.

"Boy," Sam said slowly, "we won't waste time arguing your squatter's rights —"

"This is a legal homestead!" Gutierrez broke in hotly. "It is you who step out of bounds!"

"You're leaving," Sam continued tonelessly. "We've decided that."

Gutierrez laughed bitterly, swept his hand in a wide gesture. "How far does cattleman's greed go? — onto the burned-out roof of hell itself? Look — this creek branch ran dry years ago — the grass of these flats all die . . . the Spanish Spade abandon this range, no?"

"Then why bother to file here?" Sam countered flatly. "To spit in our eye?"

"No," flared Gutierrez. "I see where I can dig small canal for a hundred yards from the main stem of Tie Creek, start the dry streambed flowing again. I would run ditches into my fields and —"

"No matter. You got any stuff in the house, in the sheds, get it out. We'll see you to your horse."

"Hold on." Leather creaked as Milo Squires swung his bulk from saddle; he threw his reins and tramped over to them, holding his enigmatic half-smile. Chet Bannerman followed with thumbs tucked in his belt, grinning his wolfish delight.

Sam eyed Milo narrowly. "What's on your mind?"

"You're too soft. This pepperbelly's got a mean eye. I know his sort. He'll be back."

"We're doing it my way, Milo."

"Don't recall anyone electing you leader. And this is Spanish Spade land, remember?"

Gutierrez' rebellious, angry stare swung suddenly on Paddy Delaney. "Does the law stand now with those who laugh at law? Answer me that, Mister Deputy . . . Mister Cattleman's Deputy!"

Paddy scowled, troubled gaze lowered to the ground as though he hadn't heard.

"This business is no part of his jurisdiction," Sam said, his tone clipped and harsh. "I asked him along to see no one gets hurt. You hear that, Milo?"

He turned back to the stocky Spanish Spade ramrod — stiffened. Squires had palmed out his gun, and it was leveled at Sam's stomach. Sam's quick glance found Chet, saw that he had quietly maneuvered behind Paddy and MacLaughlin and was covering them both.

"Now," Milo Squires said gently, "we do it Spanish Spade's way. We aim to serve the pepperbelly a lesson that'll stick."

CHAPTER TWO

Sam Ashby hauled a deep breath and let it out. He made his words reasonable: "You got authority for this from General Bannerman, Milo?"

Squires smiled, shrugging his gunhand in a semi-circle. "Genril said, take any steps I figure need taking . . . sort of hinting your idea didn't go far enough. We do it your way and them other sodders who been eyeing our open range hear about it, they'll figure they was scared of a big bluff. You want to bluff, all right, only back it all the way. Little rough stuff now'll head off a lot more later on. Now drop them cutters, boys . . . that's it."

He stepped back a few paces, now covering Boone MacLaughlin and the deputy as well. "Chet . . . ought to be a coal-oil lamp inside. You got matches?"

"No," whispered Gutierrez. "All I own in the world. . . ."

"Chili-picker, I do admire your gall. But you ain't half-growed. A man now, he makes a gamble, he's set to pay his losses. And boy — you lost."

Chet sheathed his gun and chuckled with a note of pure mirth, wheeling to head for the shack. Gutierrez didn't hesitate; he sprinted three long strides, grabbed young Bannerman by the shoulder, spun him about and drove a bony fist into his mouth. Chet staggered a long backward step, lost footing and skidded on his rump in the dust. Face distorted with rage, he clawed for his pistol.

Milo, still smiling, tilted his gun upward and fired into the air. The report whipcracked coldly across the hot tableau, halting Chet in mid-movement. He lay on his back, blinking foolishly.

"Mex, step back here," Milo ordered, and Gutierrez obeyed, his face pale and his fists closing and unclosing. Chet stood gingerly, picked up his hat and batted it across his brush chaps. He touched his bleeding mouth and lifted a raging stare to the Mexican. "Now that gets you an extra lesson."

He tramped into the shack, and through the open doorway Sam saw him pick up a lamp that centered the puncheon table, fling it against the wall. It shattered and a coal-oil stain spashed darkly across the wall and streamed down to the floor. Chet, fumbling in his fury, got out a match and struck it alight on his thumbnail, tossed it into the reeking ruin of the broken lamp. Flame mushroomed, curled up the wall. Chet stepped to the door, watching till half the partition was ablaze, and turned then with his face queerly twisted.

"Take off your shirt," he told Gutierrez. "Down on your belly. In the dirt, damn you, where you belong. . . ."

"Better do as he says," Milo Squires advised with total unconcern; his voice hardened only when Gutierrez did not move. "Ain't a court in the territory would blame me for busting up a Mex."

Gutierrez's face was a mask as he shrugged out of his shirt. Thin pliant muscles stirred beneath his dark skin as he crouched, then stretched out on his face. Chet moved forward, unbuckling his belt, and Sam found himself suddenly shaking with rage . . . but there was the steady threat of Milo's gun.

Chet stood above the prone Mexican, belt swinging from his fist as he paused fever-ishly to savor the full pleasure of it. Then his eyes flicked upward; he straightened.

"Milo . . . someone coming."

Sam traced the horizon to a moving dot . . . a rider fast-coming, the dust of his passage visible even at this distance. Milo's narrow gaze did not leave Sam as he murmured, "Who is it?"

"Christ, he's way too far to make out!" Chet snapped querulously.

Milo slowly turned his head, but still watching Sam, and then he shot a backward glance over his shoulder. At once Sam lunged in a sweeping stride — Chet yelled warning. Sam was still four feet from Milo as the ramrod swung back, and in a straining desperation Sam flung out a long arm and chopped blindly at Milo's wrist. The calloused edge of his palm jolted the arm down; the heavy gun discharged into the ground. Sam's lunge carried him full into Milo and he caught Milo forearm in both hands and smashed it across his lifted knee.

Milo let out a bull-bellow of pain, dropping the gun, and then Sam butted his shoulder viciously against Milo's thick chest and heaved him staggering away. Sam bent; in one motion he scooped up the gun, wheeled about and saw that Paddy must have moved when he did, retrieving his gun which was now trained on Chet.

MacLaughlin bent and picked up his old

.44 Colt. Sam noted with cold anger the same sullen indifference on MacLaughlin's face that had marked it when Milo took over. But he forgot MacLaughlin, glancing first at Chet, afterward at Milo Squires who stood flat-footed, rubbing his wrist. The feral rage mounted uncontrollably in Sam and battered down his usual stolid restraint. He walked over to Paddy and handed him his gun, then turned to young Bannerman and slapped him savagely across the face, cuffing him again on the backswing.

The second blow staggered Chet as his jaw fell in shocked surprise from the first. He backed away, his hands raised. "Don't!" he cried shrilly. "No more —"

"Sonny," Sam said thickly, "you're right. Man shouldn't waste drawing breath to blow you over."

"Sam, for God's sake —" Paddy got out in strangled objection, but Sam had already pivoted on his heel and was walking straight for Milo Squires. Milo re-formed his grin and braced his feet, and then Sam drove at him. The force of his rush carried them into Milo's horse which snorted and shied away. They plunged into the dirt, Sam wrapping an arm around Milo's neck and driving long, slogging blows into his face.

Milo merely grunted and dug his chin into

his chest so that Sam's punches knuckled harmlessly against his hard skull. He threw his thick arms around his opponent and tightened them. Sam pitched his weight to roll them on their sides, arching his body against the choking hug. He wedged his palm beneath Milo's chin and forced Milo's head back, inch by inch, to a pain-wrenched angle.

With an explosive grunt Squires gave up and let go, rolling catlike to his feet. Sam was up and after him at once, crowding him relentlessly. For a while they slugged it out toe to toe, till weariness dragged at their limbs. Sam hardly realized that his arms were weighted like lead, that his battered ribs ached with gusty breathing, his face bruised and bleeding. Milo Squires was a born brawler, but he couldn't stand against this raw, dogged fury. He knew he was giving Sam the worst of it, yet the lean rancher kept boring in the more savagely. Milo panicked and gave back a step, throwing up his arms to protect his face, and Sam's fist sank into his belly. Milo buckled, dropping his hands to his middle, and Sam hit him in the face.

Squires struck the dirt and rolled to his hands and knees, then scrambled up and ran to a mattock which leaned against the shack wall. He fisted both hands around the handle and stood spraddle-legged as Sam came after him.

Sam half-ducked under Milo's savage swing, catching it on his shoulder so the blunt iron bounded off at an angle. Then he was inside Milo's guard and he grabbed the mattock above Milo's grip and drove in his heels, forcing Milo's shoulders against the wall. The boards were hot, smoke wisping from their cracks, and Milo cried out. Abruptly he let go the mattock and threw a punch which caught Sam high on the forehead. Sam leaped back and swung the tool like a club. It slammed Milo alongside the neck and he staggered away, cringing behind his raised hands.

Sam tossed away the mattock and lurched after the Spanish Spade man. He battered Milo's hands down and drove a left hook to the point of his jaw that snapped the ramrod's head back. Squires' knees hinged, and Sam stepped aside to let him drop on his face.

Milo rolled on his back, gleaming eyes slitting from swollen flesh. They held no fear, only a chilling hatred. He lay with his shirt half torn off, the pale skin beneath mottled with bruises, his great chest laboring for air.

"Too — tired," he gasped. "Or I'd — finish it — finish you."

Sam stood above him, hands loose at his sides now, his anger exhausted. He glanced at Paddy, and the deputy shook his head once, almost sorrowfully. Wordlessly he handed Sam his gun.

Gutierrez stood buttoning his shirt. For the first time he displayed a wariness edging on fear, and it was Sam that he watched.

Ashby took a step on unsteady legs, shook off Paddy's offered hand and plodded to the water trough. He bent and dipped up a hatful of water, dumped it over his head. The wet coolness cut through his numb exhaustion, aroused him to alertness and a score of throbbing aches. He dried his face on his bandanna and straightened, turning a speculative stare on the approaching horseback rider, who was much nearer now. All of them were silent, watching the coming rider as though with distracted relief from what had just happened.

When the rider was still yards away, Sam realized that it was a girl, riding astride like an Indian woman, her dark skirt billowing in the wind. She drew up her lathered horse with a strong hand and slid easily to the ground, came straight up to Sam with a brisk, swinging stride. She was a tall girl, tall as the average man; the dark crown of her hair, wind-blown and tangled, came to the bridge of his nose. She glanced past him at the house. The roof had caught flame; smoke gushed from the windows and doorways.

"You are satisfied, Mr. Ashby?" Passionate venom edged her tone. "Or maybe you hang him now — hang the greaser boy?"

Sam said narrowly, "I don't know —"

"I am Celsa Gutierrez. His sister. Early this morning a friend came to me, saying there is talk of what you plan to do."

The Mexican grapevine, Sam wearily knew. "Think you could stop it?"

"No." Pure contempt seared her snapping eyes. She was sturdy, slender but not soft, in the rough duck-jacket she wore over a high-necked blouse. Her face was strong-boned, with fine, sharply angled features like her brother's, surely not pretty. But the defiant, independent pride that burned there held Sam Ashby's reluctant attention. If it was strange to find this quality in a peon boy, it was stranger by far to see it blaze in a Mexican woman. As a rule the Spanish-Indian temper either lay dormant, else burst with volatile abruptness; in this girl it burned like a steady flame, controlled and yet fierce.

Sam suddenly felt as abashed as a schoolboy with ten thumbs. He shifted his feet, scrubbing his palm over his chin. He gestured aimlessly at the fire. "Not of my making," he muttered.

"Ashby and I tried to stop that, Miss Gutierrez," Paddy put in lamely. "Sam, he just wanted to —"

"Never mind," Sam declared harshly, his awkwardness under control. "Why did you come, then — to beg?"

Deep anger flushed Celsa Gutierrez' face; a vein pulsed in her throat. Yet she said softly, "To beg, gringo? Oh no. One thing I don' do — not to you or anybody. If I had think to bring a gun, I would shoot you . . . of this be sure. But I never beg!"

She walked past him toward her brother, ignoring them all as though they'd ceased to exist. Vicente lowered his head and toed at the ground, obviously deeply ashamed . . . whether of being defended by his sister or of being driven from his claim, it was hard to say.

"Celsa," he mumbled, *"es una verguenza —"*

"A mi que," she said irritably. *"Es probable que suceda."* She took his arm and marched him firmly toward the tool shed to salvage what remained of his possessions.

Chet, darting a fearful glance at Ashby,

helped Milo Squires to his feet and over to his mount. Milo got a toe in stirrup and heaved himself across his saddle, his face nearly bowed against the mane. His eyes were almost sick with hatred. "Sam," he whispered, "I'll be seein' you."

Sam started to reply and checked it; under the circumstances, it would have been a gesture, and he had contempt for all gestures. He moved between Paddy and MacLaughlin, stood iron-faced as the Spanish Spade duo rode away. MacLaughlin muttered, "I'll be going too."

Sam said nothing. Boone tramped to his horse, mounted and paused to survey the blazing shack. The fire was well advanced, curling and crackling smokelessly around the black clean char beneath. His face impassive, Boone put his horse into motion, and Sam watched him go. Then he caught Paddy's eye; the deputy looked pale and shaken still.

"There's things I'm just learning about you, Sam," he said slowly.

Sam lifted his shoulders, let them fall. "Let's get out of here." His tone was surly, and Paddy discreetly said no more.

Something like his usual no-nonsense calm was restored to Sam as they rode through the bright morning. He said presently: "I never saw her before."

Paddy started, aroused from a bleak brown study. "Her? — oh, the girl. She's a strange sort. Maverick, I guess you'd say, a loner. . . ."

"A Mexican girl from the shanty-town? I made her age twenty-four or -five, anyway. Most of 'em are married when they're sixteen with a kid or two. . . ."

"Not this one. She's got a mind of her own. Moved out of Mextown a while back, lives on the edge of Elkhorn in an old rail-worker's shanty she fixed up. Waits on tables in Ma Jagger's Cafe." Paddy lapsed into brooding silence, finally bursting out: "This was a stinking business, Sam."

"That's why I wanted to get it over fast." With a rare hint of affection, Sam slapped the deputy's shoulder. "Come on, you redheaded Mick. The warbag's sewed up."

Paddy forced a grin. "And you'll go home to a loving wife and a good meal, while I'm after returnin' to bachelor's hell. . . ."

"Reminds me. You're invited to supper, out of my pure selfishness. Nancy'll be chewing my ear till the sun goes down, and damned if I'll stick it out alone."

"Alone, eh? Man, I didn't tell Whit McKeogh about this. Hard to say how he'll take my siding you. . . ."

Sam shrugged, a faint sarcasm in his voice: "If I know the sheriff, he'll just quote some book at you. Tell him the truth, you came along to stop trouble."

"Sure," Paddy said wryly. "Sure. Now if I could believe it myself. . . . At any rate, the prospect of one of your Nancy's fine meals will bear up my spirits; there's a cheery thought."

They reached the town road and parted shortly afterward, Sam taking a fork-off to his ranch and Paddy heading on to Elkhorn.

CHAPTER THREE

Paddy Delaney's father had been one of the many wild, roistering Black Irishmen who had swarmed West in '68 to lay track for the Union Pacific. Like most of his compatriot rail workers, Mike Delaney had an appetite for a good fight; unlike most, he'd been possessed of a fierce and driving ambition that had soon carried him to ownership of a middling-sized ranch in Two Troughs Basin. He'd stood shoulder-to-shoulder with that early-settler breed that had fought Indians and rustlers to tame a land. On a night two years ago, he'd gotten roaring drunk in Elkhorn, and while returning to his ranch bawling a lewd ballad, he had ridden his horse into the spring-swollen creek and was drowned.

Paddy had promptly sold the ranch and moved to town, arguing Sheriff Whitley McKeogh into giving him a job. His motherless boyhood of following lonesomely in his father's brawling rootless steps had left him ingrained with an overwhelming longing for stability and security. He looked forward to the day when Two Troughs Basin would be carved into tilled fields, when tough Elkhorn would banish the last of its saloons and brothels for schools and churches.

He'd tried to analyze his deep friendship with Sam Ashby on that basis, could only guess that it stemmed from Sam's great likeness to his father, whom he had loved and respected . . . and feared. Just as, after this morning, he now feared Sam a little. Paddy could never understand men like his father and Sam, outwardly so different, inwardly incredibly alike with their single-minded devotion to their self-hewed destinies, their capacity for sudden, raging violence against anything that blocked their own iron decisions. Yet with such men their given word was their bond; they tempered their hard-bitten independence with a deep loyalty to friends and family, with high standards of personal integrity; they were always the first to enter a land, and their kind died hard in the face of change. They had scant patience for the laws of society, which they did not break wantonly but simply disregarded when these laws contravened their own ends.

They were men who could stand alone, and make other men feel their strength.

And with that strength, Paddy knew guiltily, they could dominate their quieter, more sedentary friends. "A stinking business," he'd said of the job this morning, of which he'd been squeamish from the first. Paddy Delaney was quietly certain that a peacefully settled and developed basin would come only when the old order was overthrown, when many little homesteads of decent, conventional people replaced the handful of wide-flung ranches and their hard back-country breed of loners like Sam Ashby. Yet he'd gone meekly along with Sam and only partly for friendship's sake. In matters big and small, Sam's personality, with a kind of frightening ruthlessness, overrode his.

Paddy's thoughts were troubled now as he slumped in his chair comfortably full of Nancy Ashby's good cooking while he brooded at the red-and-white checked tablecloth. Nancy glanced up from her sewing and smiled.

"Why so quiet, Paddy?"

Paddy's round face assumed a smile and a cheery wink. "Why, darlin', I was mulling schemes to the end of enticin' you off to my dreary bachelor's quarters, there to ever after prepare me matchless dinners."

Sam, an arm thrown over the back of his chair while he swirled the dregs of his coffee and stared absently into the cup, looked up with only a perfunctory smile at this banter. Supper had been a strained affair, Paddy reflected, breached by the cold silence that had held between the Ashbys since his arrival. There'd certainly been a family squabble he hadn't seen, and he wasn't surprised — Nancy Ashby was strong-minded in her own right, and she was of Paddy's opinion in the homesteader matter, as were most of the basin women.

Nancy gave her full, hearty laugh and stood up. "I'll freshen your cup, Paddy."

"Not too much coffee for Paddy," Sam cautioned with a smile that only partly tempered his dry tone. "Tomorrow's Sunday, he'll need a good night's sleep to be up in time for church."

"That's right," Paddy agreed, round face flushing in spite of his ready grin. Punctually on every Sabbath morning, Paddy arrived at the little mission over in Mextown for eight o'clock Mass. The Mexicans had been at first startled to find an Americano who would openly share their faith in their place of worship, and they still greeted his weekly arrival with an air of wondering, yet pleased, surprise. . . . The basin ranchers, with joshing condescension, had built a community church for their womenfolk in Elkhorn, but Preacher Paley's hell-fire sermons found few of the men in regular attendance.

Nancy spun away from the cupboard with fire in her eye. "It wouldn't hurt you at all to follow his example now and then!"

"All right," Sam said wearily. "I'll take you to church tomorrow. Does that make you happy?"

"Not when you offer to in that way."

"What way, for God's sake!"

Paddy blinked his embarrassment. That earlier squabble must have been a true Donnybrook. Nancy now simply nodded at Paddy, then darted a fierce look at her husband.

Sam sighed, lifted a big hand and dropped it flat on the table. "Sorry, Paddy."

Paddy chuckled nervously. "That's all right, folks . . . makes a man feel right at home." His feeble play dropped like a stone into the strained atmosphere as Nancy refilled his cup from the big cow-camp coffeepot. "Well, I'd best be going soon," Paddy muttered and gulped the steaming brew; he barely bit back a curse as he scalded his tongue.

"Take your time," Sam said harshly, as he came to his feet. He stalked to the door, paused to lift his hat from a rack of staghorns and added more quietly, "Reckon Nance would like to talk a bit. It's a far piece from town and you don't come out often enough, boy. I got to see to a couple chores . . . you better be here till I get back anyway."

It was Sam's indirect, yet bluff, way of apology, Paddy knew, and he beamed his relief. "Surest thing you know, Sam."

Sam closed the door and his boots thumped solidly across the porch. There was a moment's silence, then Nancy cleared the dishes from the table and carried them to the battered wreckpan that was a relic of Sam's open-range bachelor days. Paddy watched her back with troubled eyes. She was a fine figure of a woman, he thought a little wistfully, plump and sturdy as befitted a hard-working ranch wife — still with more than a hint of girlish prettiness, though she was in her late twenties. Paddy, the only close friend of both Ashbys, knew better than anyone the deep need and affection between them, that part of their marriage which no surface discord could touch. Yet he was disturbed by what he'd witnessed tonight, for he was familiar with the mutually stubborn minds of both that could divide them so hopelessly.

There was a full ten minutes of silence before Paddy said finally and awkwardly, "Nance, it's truly sorry I am to see you and Sam at loggerheads. If there's a thing I can do — or say — that'll ease matters. . . ."

Nancy turned, tossing her head to throw back an auburn curl from her forehead. She smiled wanly. "It'll be all right, Paddy." She hesitated. "And yet — you're his friend — our friend . . . you know how I hate this whole mess. The country is changing, and the times we live in — and he won't see it! He's so mulish set in his ways . . . like a bull trying to tear the ring from his nose! He'll surely hurt himself — and others . . . I can see it coming. Oh, Paddy —"

She began to cry softly, and Paddy felt a confused alarm. "Here, now . . . that won't do." He got up and went to her, taking her by the shoulders. "Nance, he's devil of a hard man to understand; no one knows that better than myself. But we've got to be tryin', you far more than I. For his sake and your own."

She raised her face quickly, wiping her eyes. "I know. I know. I will, Paddy." She

43

summoned a smile. "I suppose he's gone to mope somewhere. Well, I won't put it off . . . I'll find him now and we'll get the thing talked out."

"Good for you," Paddy grinned and rose to walk to the antler-rack, reaching for his jacket and shrugging into it. "In that case, I'll not be waitin' on Sam's return. Give him my regards. . . . Bit of a chill, tonight."

Nancy took down an old blanket-coat, and Paddy quickly moved to help her slip it on, despite her smiling protest. "Honestly . . . you spoil a woman terribly."

"One of my few shortcomings," Paddy chuckled. "Say now, isn't this Sam's old coat?"

"Oh, I like it for outside chores . . . it's the warmest one we have." As Nancy spoke she moved back to the table to turn down the lamp.

A pane of the little window at her back exploded in a shower of glass, merging with the whipcrack of a rifle shot. Nancy jerked, half-turning. A pan clanged to the floor from a wall hook, bent by the slug.

Nancy leaned both hands on the table, her face strangely twisted, a deathly saffron in the lampglow. "Paddy —" He leaped to catch her as she fell, easing her gently to the floor. He felt a sick shock at a hot wetness puddled against her back and jerked his hand away — only then saw the dark soaking of her bodice where the coat fell open. The bullet had taken her squarely in its path.

"Get . . . Sam."

"Mother of God," Paddy whispered.

"Paddy . . . get him . . . get Sam . . . hurry. . . ."

And then Paddy understood and he ran blindly out the door, across the porch and the moonlit yard. "Sam!"

No answer. Paddy dashed wildly through deep shadows that masked the big grindstone by a stacked pile of slabs, tripped over it headlong. Scrambled up and veered on around the corner of a hay shed — "Sam!"

But it wasn't Sam, that figure of a man cutting off toward a little stand of cottonwoods at a furtive run and then lost to sight in the shadows.

"Murdering spalpeen!" Paddy blistered out a fierce Gaelic oath and yanked his gun from holster, racing toward the point where he'd seen the skulker vanish. He heard the low whicker of a horse from the cottonwood grove and with desperate haste he plunged down a brushy aisle, flailed his way through and burst into a moon-dappled small clearing.

He had a single confused glimpse of the horse standing there — and then a purple-orange flame spewed waist-high to a dark shadow alongside it.

The slug's impact flung Paddy about like a rag doll. Sight and sound and feeling ribboned off and he never heard the second shot.

Sam Ashby stood alone at the end of the horse pasture, well beyond the last outbuilding. He leaned his back against the fence poles, an arm hooked over one of these, breathing deeply of the chill wind that hailed down from the Elks to the north, bearing with it the smell of snow-locked heights and of greening spring picked up on its deep dip through the warm basin night. He shivered with its icy breath, but it was good against his cut and aching face.

Solitude and a sense of natural things was Sam Ashby's balm when all else failed him . . . as it occasionally did, even after half-a-dozen years of marriage. There were deep and lonely wells in him that Nancy, with all her great capacity for soothing his bad moments, could not touch. Born with that little-boy lostness that sometimes lurked below his tough, self-sufficient exterior and yet was a part of it. Always he's stared with cold realism into the eye of life, making no effort to cushion its impact with self-delusions, a quality that could badly shake a man at times.

Yet . . . Nancy had been good for him. So much so that at times he felt an awed humility before her love and understanding. Both had been older than most who were joined in frontier wedlock, on that day six years ago when they were wed simply and quietly in the parlor of her parents' home in Omaha by Nancy's father, a judge.

Both had brought to their marriage a deeper knowing — of life, of joy and heartbreak — than most, and if their courting had been a trifle lengthy and cautious, it had established a bond that made Sam wonder how he had been able to live twenty-six years without it. It now seemed as essential to his being as eating or breathing. There had been no children, and this was a single mar, leaving its small emptiness of which neither ever spoke . . . but Sam couldn't imagine returning to his wild youth as a thirty-and-found trailhand — dust-choked, grueling cattle drives up from Texas . . . a drunken, brawling kaleidoscope of days and nights in the wide-open rail-head towns . . . waking full of a bad taste and worse regrets . . . only to start the vicious circle all over.

Sam had always been searching, for something to fill the stark memory of an orphaned youth, and his marriage had made the difference. All the difference in the world, now. The man he'd been might have joined in with wolfish eagerness this morning when Milo Squires and Chet Bannerman had set themselves to beat that Gutierrez boy . . . perhaps to near-death, if he knew Chet. Milo was older and shrewder, a more complex individual, yet of the same mean mold.

But Sam Ashby wasn't that man any longer. Thank God for that, and her.

Abruptly he noted the last twilight mingling with a pre-storm murk, and he caught a distant rumble of thunder. Bleak, low-banked clouds were scudding the horizon, piling to vast thunderheads. Better get Paddy started for town before it breaks, Sam thought and headed for the house.

He'd covered half the distance when he heard a rifle shot. More puzzled than alarmed, he quickened pace. He caught a faint shout . . . Paddy's voice, he thought, and now broke into a run. There was a staccato bark of two more shots — a pistol now. Sam's long legs drove him in loping strides toward the silhouetted outbuildings. Suddenly he heard a pulse of hoofbeats off by the cottonwood grove — hauled up in his tracks, listening.

". . . Paddy?"

The only reply was the hasty sound of the horseman's going, dying away swiftly in the night. Sam moved on toward the house, his apprehension deepening when he saw Paddy's horse still tied at the rail in front, picked out by a spill of lamplight from the wide-open doorway. He hurried inside. . . .

Seconds later his two cowhands, fat Nels Nelson and little Shorty Davis, burgeoned breathlessly through the door. Nels huffed in first, struggling to slip his pants suspenders over his underwear.

"We was in our bunks, Sam — shots roused us out —" Nels stopped dead in his tracks — his jaw sagged. Sam crouched by the table, his back to them; they hadn't at first noted the limp burden he held in his arms.

"O Jesus," Nels whispered.

Only then did Sam look at them, and the two men flinched from what they saw in his face.

"Delaney's horse is still out there," Shorty muttered. "He's around some'eres. Maybe we should find him?"

Sam didn't reply, his eyes full of blank

shock not seeing them, and the two men left quickly. Sam did not note their going, aware only of the still form that he supported with her head against his shoulder. He's stanched the flow of blood but made no effort to move her, knowing it was useless. A deep and terrible fear that he had never known gripped Sam Ashby. . . .

Nancy moaned and her eyes flickered open, dimly but holding their loving recognition of him. "Sam. . . ." And she smiled.

"Don't try to move, dear. Don't talk. You'll be all right."

"Sam. . . ." Her whisper faltered and sank, strengthened briefly. "It's good you're here. We couldn't leave each other that way . . . not with our last word a quarreling one. It was never that way between us, Sam. . . ."

"You'll be all right, dear," he murmured, while the fear built steadily in him, a helpless and engulfing thing that screamed in his mind, that he could not fight.

Ashby stood on the little knoll back of the house, the place where Nancy had loved to sit. He knew that only a few minutes had passed since he'd left the covered bodies of his wife and friend laid out in the parlor, but he did not know why he'd come to this spot and did not care, only standing with his face to the rising wind. His body moved or functioned to the command of sensory impression. It did not seem numb, only curiously detached from a dead brain.

The first fat raindrops began.

"Sam."

Nels and Shorty were suddenly at his side, and it meant nothing at all. "Sam," Nels said again and swallowed painfully. "Startin' to rain. Come along now . . . we'll get you inside."

Then Shorty said something. The words drifted into Sam's mind which automatically rejected them as meaningless. A minute later he realized that he was alone and torrential sheets of rain were buffeting his body.

The animal part of him shivered and was cold, and without conscious volition it turned and plodded toward the house. The lightning danced and flickered and thunder rolled deafeningly. The bursts of white light and sporadic noise drove a first wedge of wakening thought into his brain, and with it a flicker of purpose.

Before he reached the house, he had veered in his tracks, heading for the harness shed and his saddle.

The lights of Elkhorn were visible from a high ridge where he halted his mare an hour later. The town was situated toward the southern extremity of the basin, crowded into a wide wedge between the first steep foothills of the Elks. Largely by habit, Sam guided his mount down the densely timbered slope, following the ridge road. The night was impenetrably black, and slickerless, he was soaked to the skin by gusting torrents and bitterly chilled, his body numb from the beating rain. But his mind was working again, coldly battering through a dead apathy of utter grief, driving toward decision. It welcomely diverted his attention, putting off the time he'd be forced to the head-on acceptance that tonight his life had been wrecked, smashed forever by a single bullet.

Three men.

Vicente Gutierrez, proud and rebellious, against whom he'd led the party that had burned Gutierrez' claimshack and forced him off.

Chet Bannerman, the weak and spoiled son of a strong father, a bully by instinct and a coward by nature, whom he'd viciously cuffed into a groveling posture.

Milo Squires, whose fanatical pride in his domineering strength slumbered thinly beneath his bland pleasantry, whom Sam Ashby had beaten to the ground and humiliated in front of four witnesses.

He knew of no other immediate enemies, and it was hard to believe that any of these three had motive enough for a bushwhack-murder . . . but was there any other answer?

The killer must have arrived moments after Sam had left for the pasture, tethering his horse in the grove and working in close to the house . . . waiting and watching for his chance. Nancy in Sam's coat, the old blanket-coat with its distinctive black-and-green Indian design on a rusty faded background that everyone in the basin had seen Sam wear for years, had moved against that small lighted window by the table. The killer, glimpsing only that bulky coat and not its wearer, had fired at once. Then was forced to shoot Paddy when the deputy had gone after him. But it was Sam he wanted, not them.

Three men, and one of them had killed his wife and best friend. Sam's mind closed irrevocably around that decision and hugged it as a drowning man would a chunk of driftwood.

The road that led through Elkhorn wended on down a creek forking to Mextown, and there he would begin . . . with Vicente Gutierrez. . . .

Sam rode past the clutter of mean shacks

on the south side of the railroad track and cut into the heart of town, down Jackson Street with its flanking rows of false fronts. The storm, its first surcharged violence now slackening away, had long since driven town people indoors, and the lateness of the hour would keep them there. Yet Sam was alert as he paced unhurriedly down the main street.

As he came parallel to Otto Stodmeier's saloon, a sear buffet of lightning whitely polished the weathered building fronts, laying a noonday brightness across the entire scene. It picked out the single horse standing hipshot at Otto's tie rail, its rump softly shimmering in the slanting wetness. For an instant Sam saw the Spanish Spade brand clearly etched on its left hip, and as the darkness washed back he reined his horse aside so viciously that the animal stumbled. He dismounted with thunder filling his ears and trembling the earth . . . slipped his rifle from its scabbard. Stepping onto the rainglistening sidewalk, he slipped, caught his balance and shouldered through the swing doors.

He blinked against the light, stood with the water streaming off his boots and puddling on the floor planks.

Milo Squires' slickered form was slumped

across a table with his head resting on his folded arm, his fist gently cradling a near-empty bottle. His breath made a heavy, stertorous sound and the breath bubbled from his open mouth.

Sam looked at the Mexican swamper who was sweeping fresh sawdust across the floor, busily bent to his labor with his back to Sam.

"Paco. . . ."

Paco Morales turned, a heavy-set youth with gentle dark eyes and a dreamily distant smile. His brown face shown with perspiration. "Ah . . . Meester Sam. Meester Stodmeier have gone home early, and I am closing the place."

Sam gave a bare nod at Squires. "How long he been here?"

"Oh, he is getting very drunk, *borracho*. He pass out."

"How long, I said!"

Paco's eyes jumped; they grew round. "Maybe an hour. No less, for sure. He get very drunk —"

An hour . . . and not over fifteen minutes had elapsed between the killer's departure and Sam's. Too long . . . way too long.

Sam violently turned on his heel and was gone.

CHAPTER FOUR

It wasn't only Celsa Gutierrez' hard-core streak of independent pride that had prompted the final decision to leave the little sequestered settlement of her birth and buy a rundown old rail-worker's shanty on the outskirts of Elkhorn. Mexican women were expected only to marry young — and not to have opinions of their own. Celsa's wholehearted failure to conform had made her a pariah among her people. The Americans were only slightly more open-minded, and she'd known in advance that among them the stigma of race would additionally brand her. But since her natural turn of mind was solitary, though marred by an aching loneliness she could never exactly define, she'd found a certain acid satisfaction in also asserting it into a physical fact. She lived alone, returning only occasionally to Mextown to visit her only friend, her young cousin Rosa. Celsa Gutierrez earned

56

her own way, asked for nothing and gave much.

When she thought about it at all, she supposed her generosity was simply habit. She and Vicente had been orphaned in childhood by a smallpox epidemic, and Celsa, three years her brother's elder, had found herself at once an older sister, a mother and father, and a breadwinner. It had been bitterly hard, but never once had she accepted a penny, a crust of bread, that she hadn't earned by hard work. Even after Vicente was old enough to share responsibility, her manner toward him had remained fiercely protective. That too was habit, she knew, and not good for Vicente. His headstrong pride was largely artificial, copied from his sister's example; though he sometimes rebelled against the shame of his dependence, more often he returned to Celsa, pleading for advice or money of which she gave freely. Knowing that she was wrong, yet continuing to lavish on him the maternal care that should have gone to a husband and children.

She had hoped that Vicente would break the bond himself, as she could not bring herself to do. His intention to file a homestead and develop a farm had given her a first real hope. Vicente had been fired with zeal for the project; perhaps at last he'd stand on his feet as a man, win his own way. She had given him money for a plow, tools and seed, and he'd spare the cost of building a dwelling to homesteading specifications by simply taking over an old, long-deserted limeshack on range that Spanish Spade no longer used. Surely the basin ranchers would not object to this.

She had been wrong . . . thanks to Sam Ashby. And then it was ruined, and Celsa could not remember an emotion as strong as her hatred for the man who had wrecked Vicente's first act of self-initiative. Vicente had returned to Mextown to sullenly mope away his mananas.

Then she'd seen Sam Ashby, for the first time since the night his wife and Paddy Delaney were murdered, and all her hatred had evaporated in a wondering pity. It was common gossip that since that time, without missing a night, Ashby had gotten deeply, stupidly drunk. When his money had run out a month ago, he'd sold his ranch and gone on a roaring binge for ten solid days and nights until someone picked his pocket as he lay in an inert stupor. Afterward he worked during the days, swamping out saloons and the livery stable, for enough to get drunk at night.

Seeing him again, Celsa had scarcely

believed that this was the alert, iron-eyed man she'd met two months before.

Sitting now in her shanty home, her faded wrapper pulled tight about her shoulders in a faint dawn chill, Celsa sipped a cup of tepid chicory and mused on it all. Gazing about the single small room which she had comfortably refurbished, she felt oddly restless, with more than usual dissatisfaction. She supposed that she was only lonesome . . . surely it would be no concession to her independence of mind to invite someone — another girl — to share her home, such as it was. They'd be a little cramped for space, but with what they could save on shared expenses they could build a couple of extra rooms . . . a parlor, and a real kitchen.

There was that new girl who had come to work at Ma Jagger's restaurant, relieving part of Celsa's workload . . . Christine Powers. Celsa had liked her at once, as she did anyone who was destitute and lonely. The girl's past so obviously contained bitter abuse, with all her desperate, withdrawing shyness like some hurt animal, that Celsa's warm impulse to help her had also crystallized the notion of bringing Christine to live with her. Yet, a dozen times on the point of asking, Celsa had bitten her tongue — her ever-assertive pride steeled against a possible rebuff. She was *india,* or mostly, for she had never believed her father's brag about his pure Castilian blood — and Christine was a white girl. Celsa's experience in such matters had ingrained her with a wary sensitivity she could not overcome.

In her restlessness she stood up, carried her few soiled dishes to the washpan, then moved quietly to the gunnysack hanging that partitioned off a third of the shack interior. She stirred it open with a raised hand, looking in on the recumbent form of Sam Ashby, stretched out on the straw pallet that ordinarily served for her own bed.

Last night she had heard a heavy form bump against her door, and when she'd opened it, Ashby lay slumped against the door outside, sunk in a drunken, unknowing stupor. Within her quickly surged wondering pity, and without hesitation she'd dragged him into her room to sleep it off. As was her fashion, Celsa hadn't asked herself whether her action was becoming or conventional; the night was chill and damp and the man had needed help.

Again she felt that wondering compassion, gazing on Ashby's face. It was slack and puffy, pale yet mottled with an unhealthy ruddiness. The thick black beard that slurred its lower outlines was of two weeks' duration, and his straight hair was long and untrimmed. His clothes were stiff with filth, and he stank of old sweat and sour whiskey. His snoring breath bubbled and rasped through his open mouth.

What could turn a man such as he into this? Celsa wondered . . . for Sam Ashby had been a man, for all her rancor against him. Her brother had told her how Ashby, though taking the worst of it, had beaten that thick bully of a *segundo* Squires into the dirt to save Vicente a beating. The event hadn't lessened Celsa's hateful resentment for the tall man. Herself of a stubborn and almost grim pride, she'd at once spotted the same quality in Sam Ashby — knew it was this that had led him to punish Milo Squires, for opposing Ashby's will.

A sudden insight crept into Celsa's thoughts. We proud and lonely ones, we always feel the deepest, are hurt the most. That was it . . . the higher one towered within himself, the farther he fell when his time came. How he must have loved his wife . . . for her death had torn the insides from the man, left him as a living corpse that walked and talked and mostly stayed drunk.

She remembered how Ashby had stormed

into her shack that night . . . demanding to know where her brother was. Celsa had rarely felt fear, but she'd known fear then . . . had somehow stammered out a lie. She'd thought for a moment he would strike her, but then he was gone. Celsa had hired a livery horse and hurried to nearby Mextown, and Rosa's house where Vicente was staying — warned him to leave. A thoughtful precaution, for after a search of Elkhorn, Ashby had ridden to Mextown and rudely invaded every dwelling in his fury to find Vicente. Since that time Vicente had been camping out, moving adroitly in and out of both settlements and quietly avoiding both Ashby and the sheriff.

But there was no longer anything to fear from Sam Ashby. His lust for revenge had died as quickly as it had flared, hopelessly baffled by utter uncertainty of the murderer's identity. The only three people with likely motives had sound alibis. The coroner's inquest had brought out the fact that Vicente Gutierrez had spent the entire evening at the home of Paco and Rosa Morales, and while Paco's wife testified for Vicente, Paco vouched for Milo Squires who had been getting drunk in Stodmeier's saloon at the time; Chet Bannerman had been playing cards in the bunkhouse at his father's ranch.

With the check of these absolving testimonies on his vengeful rage, Sam Ashby had nowhere to turn but to a bottle. Which he did.

Looking on him now, Celsa shook her head once sadly and then turned at a light rap on the door. She went to the door and lifted the latch, opening it. Vicente brushed in past her, saying without preliminary, "I need a little money. For grub and. . . ."

He broke off, staring past the pulled drape at the man on the pallet. "*Madre de Dios!* You admit that gringo, my enemy, to your bed! You — !"

"Take care of your speech," Celsa warned sharply. "The gringo fell drunk outside my door. The night was cold, and I brought him in . . . while I slept on those blankets by the stove. It was as much as I would do for a dog — even you."

Vicente swallowed, shamefaced. "Give me your pardon, *hermana mia.* I didn't think. . . ."

"This is rare?" she gibed.

He flushed, his mood shifting instantly from contrition to sulkiness. "I need money."

"Again I say — this is rare?" Celsa demanded crossly. "You have been hiding out for weeks alone; still you're twitchy as any rabbit. What do you fear? Ashby? Look at him; do you think he could harm you now if he tried?"

Her brother turned his sorry relic of a hat between his fingers, staring sullenly down at it. "That sheriff is still looking for me."

"Do you believe," Celsa said with scathing exasperation, "that the sheriff could not track you down if he really cared to? He only requested of me in a friendly way that you come in and sign a statement. The inquest absolved you of implication in the murders of Mrs. Ashby or Delaney; he only wants your own testimony to file in the record." She paused with hands on her hips, regarding him narrowly. "Or is there something you have reason to fear, something you haven't told me?"

"I've no secrets from you," he answered in an injured tone. "I'll swear by Our Lady of Guadalupe —"

"That won't be necessary," Celsa said tartly. "What is it, then?"

"I trust no Americano or his law. It would be a thing of convenience to fix a false charge on a humble peon. I will give this one no chance —"

"You fool!" she cut him off hotly. "There is no man more honest or fair than Sheriff

McKeogh . . . none of our people ever received less than justice at his hands!"

"I trust no Americano!"

Celsa sighed and gave up. She counted out a small sum from her scanty reserve of cash; Vicente pocketed it and left with a bare word of parting. She heard him kick his horse into a hasty run and soon learned why . . . a knock came at her door and she opened it to face Sheriff Whit McKeogh.

"*Buenos dias,* Celsa," he said pleasantly, removing his hat. "Wasn't that your brother just rode off with a burr under his saddle?"

"Si, senor."

McKeogh smiled wearily. "Don't go formal on me, girl. Just asking. May I come in?"

She gave a little shrug, folding her arms as she moved aside. McKeogh stooped his lofty frame through the low doorway. He was a lanky, rawboned man with a homely horse face and thin white hair neatly combed across a receding hairline which emphasized his long, prominent forehead. He wore a clean ancient black suit with a neat and rather dapper air. He wore no badge of office, but the tidy drape of his coattail did not hide the bulge of a holstered gun. He looked, as always, kindly and tired and reflective . . . but there was iron beneath

65

that benign gentleness, as Celsa knew.

McKeogh stopped short now, seeing Sam Ashby. For a moment puzzled surprise flitted across his face. Slowly then he smiled, glancing at Celsa's face, its Indian like passiveness. "A real tough kid, aren't you?" he said gently.

"I don' know what you mean."

"Sure you don't. Will you relax? I only came to ask again if you'd get Vicente to come in and see me. Sort of expressed his sentiment, though, by hitting leather like a demon when he caught sight of me."

Celsa shrugged one shoulder. "I am not my brother's keeper, Mr. McKeogh."

"Yeah, it's too bad about him," the sheriff said dryly. He looked again, long and thoughtfully, at Ashby. "Didn't come here to give you trouble, did he?"

"He fall by my door last night. I cannot let him just lay there. I do the same for a dog," she added quickly, and the sheriff smiled. "I don' think he mean me any harm . . . he don' know what he's doing any more."

McKeogh's wide lips tightened. "Yeah." He speculatively eyed the soddenly snoring man. "Listen, when he wakes up you tell him to come over to the office. I want to talk to him."

"That is an order?" she inquired with faint mockery.

"Well . . . make it sound like one, will you, Celsa?"

CHAPTER FIVE

Sam Ashby turned unsteadily onto Jackson Street and plodded down the board sidewalk, his eyes lid-narrowed against the glancing brightness of the heightening sun. His temples triphammered with a dull and aching pulse; his tongue and throat were foul and phlegmy. In the beginning, for his hard-drinking youth was years past, he'd drunk only to forget, and the morning miseries of the heavy drinker had left him prostrate and retching. In the weeks since, his hard grief had dimmed, or perhaps, numbed. Now an alcoholic craving had become itself the focus of his every waking thought. He withstood each day only because the few poor coins it yielded gave prospect of each drink-blurred night.

He paused at the water trough in front of Kirby's Mercantile and stripped off his shirt with labored, unthinking movements, shook the chaff from it — legacy of his straw bed.

This because it irritated his skin; that the shirt was also foul with grime did not concern him. He bent and scooped up a double handful of water, poured it over his head and shoulders, swiped his shirt once across his face and shrugged into the dirty garment.

Sam Ashby straightened, swiveled his bleary gaze about the street. His eyes lingered on Ma Jagger's Cafe a block down, not because he was hungry — he could not remember when he'd last wanted food. Celsa Gutierrez was just entering the place, a tall and proud-straight girl who paused to look toward him, then turned away. He vaguely wondered why she'd helped him at all, for her attitude, as she'd shaken him awake and coldly told him to leave because she had to dress for work, had been totally unfriendly. The memory was vaguely troubling, then was forgotten as his gaze slid on toward Stodmeier's saloon.

Good old Otto . . . old Otto would have a swamping job for him — and no doubt, Burkhauser would at the livery stable. It didn't really matter . . . he'd get through the day. To Burkhauser he was just cheap help . . . but Otto Stodmeier was his friend. Otto did not like his drinking, but knew that if he refused service, Sam would only buy cheap rotgut elsewhere. And Otto still chose to fuss over him, muttering Low German expletives the while, but with massive patience, week after week, putting Sam to bed in his storeroom when Sam collapsed after a nightly liquor bout.

Otto Stodmeier was his friend, and a friend was a rare solace in Sam Ashby's life these days . . . not that he greatly cared.

He started across the street, squinting down at the glaring dust, halting almost obliviously to let a big Murphy freighter wheel past him by a foot or so; the teamster cursed him savagely. He blinked in confusion, his senses knifing to brief alertness, stood in the center of the street with his brows pulling to a frown. The Guiterrez girl . . . hadn't she said something about Sheriff McKeogh wanting to see him? He looked longingly at the swing doors of Stodmeier's, thinking of its dim coolness, the yeasty mingled odor of beer and sawdust. . . . Hell . . . might as well get it over.

Sam walked on unsteady two blocks down to the new frame courthouse, swung into the sherrif's entrance. The office was a large bare room walled with gray plaster, floored by new unpainted pine boards that mingled a resinous tang with the smell of McKeogh's old pipe. The meager furnishings were clean and tidy, like the sheriff himself, a bachelor who for most of his sixty years had looked to his own wants. The big gun rack, along the south wall beside a solid oak door leading to the cell block, was immaculately dusted, the guns cleaned and oiled to a dull sheen. All other furnishings were well-worn, having been moved from Whit McKeogh's old office and being as personal to the sheriff as his right hand. Sam recognized the old hard-coal burner and the shelves of books and *Harper's* magazines behind it . . . but not till the long winter nights, when blizzards and white stillness locked the basin, did McKeogh settle down for serious reading.

Then there was the battered ancient walnut desk, its top bare except for a heap of papers precisely squared on one corner and an open day book with Whit McKeogh's gaunt head bent above it, his chin on one fist and in the other his pipe. He glanced up, wordlessly nodded Sam to the visitor's chair, and a full minute went silently by.

Sam, sprawled against the chairback with his legs outstretched, at last stirred restlessly, and McKeogh closed the book and leaned back, his swivel chair creaking. He puffed on his pipe a placid moment, his neutral gray stare flicking over Ashby.

Abruptly he said: "How long can a man go on drinking — really drinking, I mean? Big man like you, spent his life outdoors, strong constitution — he might last for years before it kills him. Which it will."

"That all?" Sam asked stonily.

"Boy, I'm just getting warmed up." The sheriff opened a desk drawer, pulled out an object and tossed it on the desk. It clattered metallically and glinted against the mote-drifted sunlight from an east window. "Paddy's badge. I want you to wear it."

Sam had been prepared for anything from this enigmatic lawman, yet his head lifted sharply, staring rheumily at the badge.

"Don't get me wrong," McKeogh added, his tone dry and thrusting. "I don't want the town drunk as deputy."

Sam sank back with a shrug, his chin sinking to his chest. "Well . . . there's those always said you were crazy."

"There's those always said you were a man," McKeogh said thinly. "Could be they were wrong on both counts."

A wicked hint of temper flared in Sam, died as quickly. He dropped his gaze and brooded at his boots.

"Let's say I'm gambling they were right about you, anyway," McKeogh continued. "I need a man. And I'll be blunt — Delaney never filled his boots. If that's harsh on the dead, I'll ease it some — Paddy Delaney was a good sort — the best in his way, and he believed in the right things. But he was no kind of lawman, would never be if he'd outlasted me in the work. That gentle streak of his got to be a downright weakness at times. In this work you're hard and you're soft, but you don't confuse the two. You don't let your friends pull you around by the nose, for one thing —"

"Damn you, McKeogh — !"

"Brought you to life, that did, eh?"

Sam ground his teeth and did not answer, and after a moment McKeogh went on quietly, "A man has to think for himself, do for himself, or he's nothing. That means living up to what he believes — not letting friendship, anything, sway him. Paradoxically, you got to believe in yourself first before you can conduct yourself for the good of all. Shakespeare put it this way: 'To thine own self be true —' "

Sam broke in rudely, "I'll leave the book stuff to you."

Faint annoyance touched the long lines of McKeogh's face. "Look at those shelves, Ashby — what do you see?"

"Books."

"Damn it, look at them!"

73

Sam let his bleary eyes range along the titles on the top shelf — 'First Principles,' 'The Origin of Species,' 'Man's Place in Nature,' 'Population: the First Essay,' 'The Complete Works of William Shakespeare,' 'The Rubaiyat' . . . a dozen others. To Sam's notion, it was all gibberish, and the shelf beneath equally so: 'The Rights of Man,' 'The Constitution of the United States,' four volumes of 'Commentaries on the Laws of England,' 'The Holy Bible,' 'The Talmud,' 'The Upanishads' . . . his eyes ached and he looked away.

"Those top shelf books are about life and man, the bottom ones about what he tries to live by," McKeogh said patiently. "All of them were written by men who were looking for answers over a lot of centuries. The answers they found are worth knowing. A man fills in the gaps, judges the points of difference, from his own experience. No man makes a show alone, not while there's a world of other people. 'No man is an island, entire of itself.' Man named Donne wrote that three hundred years ago. To understand, to share, to help — a man who learns how to do these is never alone . . . never has any doubts about what he has to do."

Sam's attention began to stray; his tongue

felt dry and fuzzy, and he thought longingly of a drink. McKeogh said suddenly: "Why did you marry your wife, Ashby?"

For a moment the sick shock of memory tided against Sam's mind; he snarled, "Why does any man? He needs a woman."

"Oh? That's the only reason you married?"

Sam regarded him almost with hatred. "No."

"The fact is you had no purpose before, and she gave you purpose. Now the bottom has dropped out of your life. And you, my friend, do not have a damned thing to fall back on. No purpose, no philosophy, no ideas or ideals — a lot of nothing. No real guts, in short."

"Goddam you — !"

"Now here's what you could do: you could do me some good. I took a header off my horse last spring, got stove-up enough so I still feel it. Can't get around easy, and Paddy handled most of my leg work. . . . By the same token, you could do the whole basin some good; I'm retiring when my present term's up, and I want a good man broken in. Finally, you could do yourself a hell of a lot of good, get your teeth into something. All you'd have to do is shove the cork in the bottle and pin on that badge."

Again Ashby was relaxing into a lethargic indifference, and seeing it, McKeogh bit out flatly, coldly: "But you won't, will you? — you besotted bum. Too proud to take help, but not too proud to take a fall in the gutter. Go on, feel sorry for yourself, wallow in it. Get over to Otto's and drink the place dry. Go on, you drunken useless bastard."

Sam's first really sharp emotion in days, a black fury, flared high in him . . . then apathetically died as he saw what the sheriff was trying to do. Dull-eyed, he stood a little uncertainly and afterward shuffled out into the hot sunlight. Unaccountably he found himself suddenly shaking. Not drinking shakes, he knew, not yet; but now he wanted a drink and badly.

He walked swiftly to Stodmeier's and went in. The big vaulted barroom was deserted. He could hear someone stirring about in the storeroom at the rear. An open bottle and a glass were set out for the first customer of the day . . . a free drink. Yet Sam did not reach for it. He leaned his elbows on the bar and rubbed a trembling hand over his face. "Too proud to take help . . . not too proud to take a fall in the gutter."

He dropped his hand to the bar, staring at his image in the heavy gilt-edged mirror above the backbar. The hell with you,

McKeogh. The hell with you. Why should that damned sheriff's words get abruptly under his skin? He could clearly see the man of whom McKeogh had spoken glaring out of the tarnished glass. A haggard, sick-eyed man in whose face was mounting a savage revulsion compounded of fury and despair. His big hand reached, fisting around the bottle. He lifted and threw it. The bottle shattered; the mirror spiderwebbed into a score of cracks and collapsed in a jangling cascade.

Otto Stodmeier waddled from the back-room. He was a rotund man with great gray mutton-chop whiskers bisecting his broad, ruddy face. He looked at Sam and at his broken mirror, blew out his cheeks. "Mein Gott, Sam. You need to do this, eh? You cannot wreck a table, maybe a couple of chairs I fashion with these hands. Instead you smash the one thing I freight in at great cost. . . ."

Sam bent his head, knuckling a clenched fist against his aching temples. "Sorry, Otto. Sorry. Pay for it if it takes a month. A year."

Swaying against the bar in his misery, he felt Otto's pudgy palm fall gently on his shoulder. He looked up slowly, meeting the old man's eyes, their infinite compassion. "Nothing under the sun ruffle you, Otto?"

"Between friends, a little broken glass is how much, eh? So." Otto patted his arm. "You now sweep up the mess, forget it. Ach." He paused, saying heavily, "Maybe a drink you want first?"

Sam pushed back from the bar, shaking his head confusedly. "Don't know. Trying to think. Trying to. . . ."

Loud voices outside, a clatter of boots, disconcerted his befuddled thoughts. Chet Bannerman stalked arrogantly through the swingdoors, shucking his gauntlets and grinning at a boisterous remark from one of the men behind him, both Spanish Spade hands. One, Chip Suggs, was a string bean of a man with the long, mournful face of a sad hound. The other, Leo Stapp, was small, with a thin gash for a mouth and the nervous movements of a spooked cougar. A pair of shiftless troublerousers, they made a proper second and third for Chet's company.

Bannerman came to the bar and slapped his gauntlets down. "A bottle give us, Herr Squarehead. Yah, goot?"

Leo Stapp wheezed a fit of laughter at Chet's burlesqued accent. Chip Suggs appeared less amused. "I dunno, Chet . . . if your Pa or Milo find out we was sojering in town whilst we was supposed to be mending fence over by Ten Mile Spring, why —"

"Hell, you're worse'n a mother hen," Chet said sullenly. His restless glance moved down the bar, only now seeing Sam Ashby. Sam's bleak stare shifted away to the wreckage of the mirror. Chet whistled. "God, will you look at that. Der drunk do dat, ach yah, Herr Squarehead?"

Wooden-faced, Otto Stodmeier ranged a full bottle and three glasses before them. Chet poured his drink, grinning sidelong at Ashby. "Join us, drunk? Yah? Nein? Rause mit you, den."

Whooping with laughter, Bannerman and Stapp swaggered to a table, trailed by somber Chip Suggs. Sam remained leaning on the bar, his thoughts tightening to focus over the battering ache of his head, the tumult of emotion that still shook him. He didn't know what was happening to him, only that he felt on the brink of a tremendous crisis to which he couldn't put a name.

The voices of the three at the table began to rise, slurred by liquor. Chip Suggs was already morosely drunk, his words the loudest: "You goddam liar, Leo . . . I never bought no calf-kneed bronc for a hundred fifty dollars! Take it back, damn you!"

"Keep down the voice, Suggs," Otto Stodmeier said in his quiet, ponderous way.

A savage irritation at the lift of noise swept Sam; he swung from the bar. "You heard him. Shut up."

Four startled faces swiveled toward his voice. Its cold bite was that of a man they remembered, the man Sam Ashby had ceased to be. Chet Bannerman laid his palms flat on the table, licked his lower lip and shoved slowly to his feet. "Walk light, drunk. You don't make big tracks any more."

Now Leo Stapp slid catlike out of his chair, yellow eyes carefully sizing up Sam Ashby. Chip Suggs remained seated, blinking foolishly.

"Don't learn very good, do you, sonny?" Sam said softly.

A memory of humiliation boiled into young Bannerman's face; pale fury blazed there. "You stinking drunken son of a bitch!"

At once Sam started forward, and Chet's anger turned to fear. Then Leo Stapp's foot swept out in a lightning motion, kicking his chair into Ashby's path. Unable to stop, Sam stumbled, and his feet, plunging for balance, tangled between the chair rungs, tripped him headlong. Even as he fell, Stapp whipped his gun out and laid the barrel viciously across his skull. The blow glanced, exploding red pain through Sam's pounding head. He hit the floor and rolled on his side, reaching blindly for Stapp's legs. He caught a wiry shank, twisted savagely. He heard Stapp's startled yelp, heard his body crash across the table.

Sam kicked the entangling chair from his legs and floundered to his feet. Chip Suggs scrambled up and threw an awkward punch at his face. Already hurt, reflex-dulled by solid weeks of drinking, Sam staggered back against the bar. At once Chet Bannerman found his courage and ran at Ashby, hitting him in the belly. Sam doubled with a grunt, and Leo Stapp bored in from the other side and rabbit-punched him. Chip Suggs stood squarely in front, his long, skinny arms windmilling slogging blows at Sam's face.

He covered his head with his doubled arms and kicked out. His boot caught Suggs on the left shin, and Chip howled in pain and danced away, clasping his knee. Leo Stapp crowded in with his head hunched and his small hard fists tattooing a wicked flurry against Sam's ribs. Sam grunted violently and raising his flexed arm drove his elbow viciously into Stapp's ear. The painful impact drove Stapp sideways across the bar, and then Otto's bungstarter rose and fell, and Stapp's eyes rolled glassily as he slipped to the floor.

Chet gave a bleating sound and retreated as Sam wheeled after him, a big fist raised. Then he swung about and broke wildly for the swingdoors. Sam halted and glanced down at Stapp, next at Chip Suggs who sat on the floor nursing his knee with a deeply injured look. Sam Ashby touched his bloody nose, felt the pain of his gusty breathing against his bruised ribs, and he felt fully alive and it was very good.

He headed for the door.

"Sam," old Otto got out, "for Gott's sake —"

Sam paused. "I got to see Whit McKeogh . . . right away." He glanced at the gilt mirror-frame, rimmed with its broken shards. "I'll tell you, Otto —" He ran his hand through his thick black hair and chuckled softly, and Otto Stodmeier just stared at him. "— I'll be payin' you for the mirror."

CHAPTER SIX

Sam Ashby closed the day book, leaned back in the swivel chair and stretched in a yawn. A dusty sunshaft cut through the south window and mellowed the scarred surface of McKeogh's old desk; it glanced brightly from the badge pinned to the breast of Sam's flannel shirt. Elkhorn was quiet this late August afternoon, and Sam was mildly pleased with a chance for idleness and reflection. In the last month Sheriff McKeogh had wisely given him little time for either.

For in those first days after he'd taken the deputy's job and flatly quit the bottle, Sam Ashby had endured his first taste of real hell. A bath and shave and clean clothes had changed the outward man without — at first — touching the inward. Three months of hard, constant drinking couldn't be shrugged lightly away. The raw craving for liquor that gnawed in his guts had become a steady nightmare that had turned him to a haggard ghost. His nights were a sleepless, sweat-drenched torment. His stomach would not take food; he lost weight, shook like a palsied man; his nerves tottered on a hair-trigger edge.

Only the driving, inbred doggedness of the man kept him from slipping back . . . that and the dominant presence of Whit McKeogh who'd kept him on the run with long grueling cross-country rides to settle any trivial matter, anything to occupy his attention, keep him in a nadir of unthinking exhaustion. Without realizing it, Sam soon found himself beginning to wolf regular meals, falling into sound and dreamless sleep. He took on hard, spare flesh, and the incessant grind, plenty of fresh air and sun, worked their slow healing of his drink-shot system.

"Don't get cocky and try to prove something," McKeogh warned him. "We've effected a cure you could toss out the window with one sniff of whiskey. I've seen it happen to other men I thought had pepper in their craw."

As much as his self-sufficient nature could yield to dependence, Sam had come to rely on Whit McKeogh. The sheriff had given little personal advice beyond what he'd said that first day, but Sam listened to every word with respect and more. In this gaunt and somehow lonely man thirty years his elder, he'd touched a kindred thing he'd found in no other.

Sam occupied his first idle minutes of this quiet afternoon trying to sort out what had happened to him. Perhaps he'd needed to hit rock-bottom before he could feel his way as a man. Perhaps he'd simply gone the limit of his capacity for grief, and the vital need to live again had framed a turning point, the brawl with Chet and his two bullies merely cementing his decision. McKeogh, and Sam's own determination, had done the rest.

Sam propped his boots on the desk and folded his hands behind his head, squinting along the shelves of books behind the coal-burner. Then he got up and took down one at random — 'First Principles,' by Herbert Spencer. He opened it and began reading. It was tough going, full of unfamiliar jargon. He struggled with the first dozen pages, read and re-read them while resorting constantly to Whit's big dictionary at his elbow. Then patches of clarity emerged here and there, and by God, he could understand what this man Spencer was trying to do, show how everything you could think of depended infinitely on everything else, pulling it all together, the sun pouring energy into the soil, the soil into plants, the plants into animals and into men. He felt an unfamiliar and exultant excitement, and he forged doggedly on through the afternoon. When twilight began to dim the room, he paused long enough to impatiently light the desk lamp, then plunged on . . . quit only when he felt a drowsy ache starting behind his eyes.

Sam leaned back, stretching his arms and grinning at himself. Then Whit McKeogh tramped in, looking sun-boiled and pleased as a kid with his first pair of long trousers. "Lord, what an afternoon. How long since I've had a day off?"

Sam smiled. "How was the fishing?"

"You know that place a mile up the creek where the water gathers slow and deep? I got a brace of catfish —" The sheriff held his palms judiciously apart.

"Cats have taken on a sight of growing since I was a kid," Sam observed. "Must be evolution."

"Evolution, hell! I —" The sheriff paused and tongued his cheek thoughtfully. "Evolution, eh?"

Sam held up the book. "Spencer," McKeogh said, and eyed his deputy speculatively. "Feel better, don't you?"

Sam, about to cynically deny it, surprised himself by nodding.

"You fell a long ways, and hard," McKeogh mused aloud. "Don't be deceived, you got a steep climb ahead. Times you'll still feel like dropping everything, saying the hell with it. But you won't. Not if you got something personal, a philosophy, to fall back on. If a man's willing to work at it, it's the one thing he can be sure of not losing in this life." A little gruffly, he slapped Sam's shoulder. "Get out of my chair. I'll take over. You get something to eat."

Sam rose and lounged to the door, paused there to say curiously, "How you ever come by all this stuff, Whit? The books, the ideas. Were you a professor of something?"

McKeogh chuckled, slacking comfortably into his worn chair-seat. "Not hardly. Was a time when most of my reading was the directions on baking-powder cans. I was a wild kid — till I was well past thirty. Then I came across a book written by a man named Thoreau. 'Walden,' it was. You'll find it on the shelf. Easy book to read; a hard one to understand. And it got me thinking, and I wanted to know more, and I never stopped. You never do stop . . . learning."

Sam nodded soberly. "I'm finding that

out. Like Paddy Delaney . . . I thought I knew him. Now I've been in his job a while, I've got to wondering . . . why did he ever become a lawman?"

"Why," the sheriff said dryly. "Paddy had a vision. He wanted to see this country civilized. He saw law and order, their enforcement, as the way to bring it on. And he was right. But the way was a wrong one for him."

Sam came back to the desk, leaned his fists on it. "Whit. I got to know. Was there anything you've held out because you didn't figure I was ready to hear it? About that night?"

McKeogh shook his head sadly. "It's rotten, son. What happened to Paddy and your wife . . . killer getting away without a trace. But that's how it was. I went over the ground, checked out every possibility. You know how it went — nothing." A long pause before he added slowly and pointedly, "Question is — now you're part of the law and see its working — can you take that? Accept it?"

Sam let out a long breath as he straightened, his face flint-hard. "I can take it, Whit," he said quietly. . . .

He ate a lonely meal in Ma Jagger's. Celsa Gutierrez was not on duty tonight, he noted with relief, for their relations had been stained and wary since he'd picked up the raveled threads of his life. Daily she took his meal order with a few words as possible, these terse and curt. Oddly that bothered him, remembering how she had taken him in that night, given up her own bed for his drunken sleep. Now he felt regretful and a little baffled.

Tonight the other waitress, Chris Powers, took his order — a small, pale, sad-eyed girl who still retreated within herself as timidly as the day she'd arrived in Elkhorn with nothing but the clothes on her back and a worn carpetbag. This job would have gone hard for her without Ma Jagger to fiercely fend off the rowdies and loafers who came in expressly to annoy the waitresses. Celsa Gutierrez could more than handle herself; Christine Powers could not. Sam curiously wondered what her background was, what lay behind the wounded, shrinking hurt in her dark eyes.

Leaving the restaurant, he paused on the sidewalk outside, smelling the cool night and picking his teeth. The town lay settled on its haunches like a big dormant cat with a score of yellow eyes probing the silent streets . . . muscle-coiled to spring in some unguarded moment. A lawman seemed to develop an extra sense for such things. Count your blessings, Sam thought with self-irritation. Things are quiet enough for now.

A sound of hoof-falls in the soft dust of South Jackson Street drew his glance. Several men were dismounting by the Black-jack Bar, and the outflow of light picked out the short, powerful form of Milo Squires clearly as he headed up the others, tramp-ing into the bar. The Spanish Spade crew was a rowdy and hard-drinking outfit who used to patronize Otto Stodmeier in order to abusively bait the ponderous old Ger-man, till Otto's large Teutonic patience broke one night and he cut loose on several of them with a bungstarter. Since then they'd tacitly avoided his place.

Sam grinned at the thought, then angled across the street to Otto's. He found the tables and the long bar completely innocent of customers or barkeeper, but a faint noise from the rear drew his attention. He crossed the room to the door of the storeroom, palmed the knob and quietly stepped inside, closing the door again. It was a large room piled with barrels and boxes. A lamp burn-ing on an upended crate picked out Otto Stodmeier, his shirt open and his vast body slumped comfortably in a hand-carved armchair. For a moment Sam was utterly baffled by the device set on a box at Otto's elbow, with a harsh thin wail echoing from a horn above a turning disc. Then he realized that the sound was a high-pitched human voice, several in unison and they were singing 'O Tannenbaum.' Otto was nodding his head gently as he listened and keeping time batonlike with one big freckled hand. He smiled at Sam and motioned him over.

"That one of those Edison talking machines?"

"A gramophone, this. A new thing, Sam. A gift from my son. Ach, many miles it is sent packed in thick cotton. My son writes that my grandchildren make the singing while a stylus cuts the groove on the disc and there the *kinder* voices are for Grandpa many miles away. Ach, so. Vunderbar."

Sam slung his hip over the corner of a crate, swinging his foot. He listened, a faint smile on his straight mouth, till the disc had played out, saying then: "Miss them, do you, Otto?"

Old Stodmeier sighed. "My Hans, ja. His *kinder* I never see. Since my frau die, it is lonely here. Yet the old man has foolish pride; here he came eight years ago to try a new life and here he stays. . . ." Otto heaved out of his chair and shuffled to a dark window, staring out with his hands clasped at his back.

"I am a native of Prussia, Sam. There the military tradition is a fierce one. But I would save lives and not take them. I am older than most students when I get at last my chance to be a doctor. I go to Vienna, Heidelberg, Strassburg. The studies I have not complete when Bismarck's army is conscripting many men for the Franco-Prussian War. I, Otto Stodmeier, say if a man must fight, let it be for something he believes. I escape across the border to Poland with my wife and boy, there work to get passage to America. So. So. Here a man breathes air strong with the wine of freedom and is what he will be because the law protects him. For this I think I would fight." He turned slowly, nodding approval toward Sam's badge. "The law is *sehr* goot, ja?"

Sam nodded soberly, his arms folded, and he said curiously: "How come you didn't get to be a doctor over here, Otto?"

"In Europe my family is rich, but here I came with pride to earn my way, and I was no longer young . . . did not then know the English words. Also Greta and I were agreed . . . our Hans, following his own wish, would go to medical school. It was

92

hard for us, the many years I worked in a Milwaukee brewery, and Greta a scrub-woman, all for the schooling of Hans." A great pride shone in the old man's face. "Hans now is a fine surgeon in Chicago. This for old Otto is enough. So."

Sam smiled, and they talked a while longer. Then Sam jerked a backward nod at the barroom. "By the way, you leave anyone on duty in there?"

"Teufel," groaned Otto. "That shiftless Paco Morales I tell to wait on bar an hour ago while I go in here where it is quiet to play my machine."

He waddled from the storeroom, Sam following, and paused to sweep a glance across the backbar. "Ach! A demijohn of strong wine he is sneaking off with." The old man spread his hands in a hopeless gesture. "What can I do with this one, Sam? Paco I like, but he is as a child, truant of his duty when I turn my back a minute. . . ."

Sam clapped him on the shoulder and headed for the door. "I'll see if I can roust him up for you."

Abruptly aware of a commotion on the street, Sam halted at the swingdoors, quartering his glance downstreet above them. A clear drift of angry shouts carried from a large knot of men gathered in front of the

93

hotel. At that moment two men stepped from the sheriff's office. One gave a raucous, feverish laugh as he tossed in his hand something that clinked metallically, and then he threw it sideways into a shadowed alleyway. Both men hurried toward the crowd.

"Sam, what happens out there?"

"Can't tell yet . . . stay here, Otto."

He parted the doors and crossed to the sheriff's office, slipping his gun from its holster. Carefully he palmed open the door and stepped inside. The lamp burned steadily on the desk, but there was no sign of McKeogh.

Cautiously he lifted his voice: "Whit!"

"Sam! Back here . . . they locked me in. Are the keys there?"

For a moment astonishment held Sam mute. McKeogh's voice echoed from the cellblock, and then Sam realized that the bright object he'd seen flung into the alley was the sheriff's key ring. "No, they —"

"Spare set in my desk, top right-hand drawer. Shag it, man!"

Sam rummaged swiftly, found the keys and sprinted into the cellblock and down to the end cell. McKeogh was gripping the bars, his face pressed to them, as Sam

fumbled the key into the lock. "Whit, what
—"

McKeogh lunged past him as the door
swung open, down the corridor to the gun
rack. He lifted down two sawed-off Green-
ers, tossed one to his deputy without looking at him. McKeogh stalked to his desk,
opened a drawer and took out a pasteboard
box labeled Double-Ought Buck. "Where
the hell were you?"

Sam told him, watching McKeogh tear
open the box and spill a cascade of brass-
jacketed shells onto the desktop. "It's as
well," the sheriff granted, "or they might've
got you, too. Here, load up."

As they broke the shotguns and loaded a
pair of shells into each, McKeogh explained
what had happened in terse, jerky phrases.

Young Mary Fletcher, the banker's daughter, had been hurrying home from the house
of a friend on the other side of town, when,
passing the alley between the mercantile
store and the milliner's, she'd heard an
agitated pair of voices babbling in Spanish.
With the rash curiosity of the young, she
had ventured into the alley, and in the yard
at the back, picked out in full moonlight,
she'd seen two men bent above a sprawled
form — the twisted, half-naked body of a
girl.

Mary Fletcher had released her terrified horror in a knifelike scream. This had brought the two men around, and she saw their faces — Vicente Gutierrez and Paco Morales. It had also brought a horde of men from nearby buildings. Vicente and Paco had taken to their heels, but hadn't gotten far before Milo Squires and the Spanish Spade crew rode them down, herded them back at gunpoint.

The situation was explosive even before McKeogh arrived from his office two blocks down. Milo Squires was egging the mob on with a vengeance. The first stunned shock had broken into a seething, concerted rage, roaring down the sheriff's protest. Four of them had swarmed on him suddenly and disarmed him; two of these took him to the jail and locked him up.

As the sheriff finished his panted explanation, he and Sam were outside, hurrying toward the hotel.

"Who was the girl?" Sam asked. "Was she — ?"

"Susan Wells, old Barney Wells's girl. Apparently raped — then strangled to death. That, and what I told you, is all I heard before they jumped me. I made the mistake of trying to reason with them. . . . Look — !"

The crowd was surging into the courtyard adjoining the hotel.

"There's a big cottonwood back there — and they aren't waiting. Neither are we. Move it!"

McKeogh did not head for the courtyard, but toward the big double doors of the hotel. They raced across the lobby and up the stairs. Loping on the sheriff's heels, Sam was mystified, and then he understood. If they look to be stopped, they'll look low, not high.

The two ran the length of the second-story corridor. At its end a window opened above the back yard. The sash was raised to admit cool air against the lingering heat of day, and McKeogh thrust his head and shoulders through above the sill. Sam crowded beside him for a sight of the lantern-lit tableau below.

The small fenced yard was crowded with men. Men in their shirtsleeves and night-robes, muttering and cursing, an ominous and suppressed violence to their limited movements. Every eye fixed on the cleared spot around a huge old cottonwood whose top limbs were lost in the darkness above. Two horses were being led into the cleared space by Spanish Spade men. Milo Squires had just finished tossing a pair of lariats over a stout limb, anchoring the ends to the trunks. Even in the passion of the moment Sam was struck by Milo's dispassionate command of the mob's raw violent fury.

At Milo's cold-clipped orders, the two Mexicans were ejected from the tight-packed throng, flung sprawling into the cleared area. Milo dragged Paco Morales to his feet and brutally half-flung him across a saddle; Leo Stapp did the same to Vicente Gutierrez. A glass-eyed, blood-drained shock held the faces of the Mexicans, as though they could not comprehend the thing that was happening. . . .

Whit McKeogh leaned far out the window, thumbing back both hammers of his Greener. His voice lashed whiplike across the swell of voices: "That's enough!"

Twenty or more startled faces swung up. Leo Stapp made a catlike grab for his holstered pistol.

"Don't do it," Sam rapped out, nosing his weapon into view past McKeogh.

A weighted stillness sank over the mob for an eternity of five seconds, and into it McKeogh dropped his next words: "It's all off, boys. Because the range is about right for these scatterguns to cut the pack of you to doll rags."

A soft southerly wind riffled the cottonwood leaves, cutting the cottony layer of tension. A man on the fringe of the crowd broke away and left quickly. Others shifted their feet and murmured.

"We just won't argue, gentlemen," McKeogh said softly. "Ones who live here get back to your homes. Rest of you get out, the damned lot — and I mean out of town!"

Strangely not a word of objection was lifted. McKeogh had a way about him, rarely shown as now, usually buried deep within the gentle, musing man they all thought of as more of a sardonic Dutch uncle than a sheriff. That way was pure steel, Sam realized. The rest dispersed un-hurriedly, something ominous still in their mingled murmurs.

Milo Squires stood his ground the long-est, his hooded stare fixed on the two law-men, before he slowly turned to the horses.

"Don't touch them," the sheriff advised, wagging the shotgun muzzle in a gentle circle. "I'll bring out your horses. You get out with the others, you sleepy-eyed bas-tard. . . . Sam, stay here till I reach the yard."

Sam nodded, moving into the position vacated by the sheriff. For a long cold mo-ment, Milo Squires' upturned eyes locked his. Milo's face was a study, and Sam could read nothing in it, nothing of the mind of this squat man with his secretive, vicious soul. And Sam thought bleakly, as Milo moved after the others, There'll be more to this thing . . . it won't rest here.

CHAPTER SEVEN

In the office an hour later, Sam lounged in the swivel chair, absently turning a pencil between his fingers and scowling at it as though he'd never seen it before. He glanced across the room where McKeogh was running a dust rag over the already immaculate gun rack and said abruptly: "Whit — what made them do it?"

"I'm not sure they did."

"I mean the people. Merchants, workaday cowhands, respectable and decent people. What made 'em explode all at once, throwing the law, justice, everything they've been taught to believe overboard in a few minutes. Happened so fast, I still can't believe it. . . ."

"What made them do it?" McKeogh repeated, walking slowly to the desk and easing a hip onto its edge. "Well, I've seen lynching fever before — but in the early days. And this is 1889. Funny, eh? We're supposed to be getting civilized . . . yet I never saw a mob action break so fast. Mostly they work themselves into a stew, and that takes a while. . . ."

"Why, then?"

"A lot of reasons. This was a bad situation sparked in a bad time. The country's tamed down . . . the people haven't. Man is still an animal, and every time in history he's got swelled up enough to forget it, his animal side, unguarded, takes over and submerges the human. Been a quiet summer, too — and people get bored. They have personal troubles. You've seen drovers tree a town after a thousand miles on the trail. Times when it tears loose in a man, it has to come out. But here's the clincher: it wasn't just that a couple of men raped and killed a woman. What really sticks in their craw is that a couple of Mexicans raped and killed a white woman."

"But you said —"

"And meant it. So far as I'm concerned, I'll need a sight more than circumstantial proof to clinch their guilt. But a conservative ninety per cent of the basin will have them convicted and hung, soon's the word has spread. Human nature being what it is, the Mexican segment will be as blindly certain that two innocent men are being railroaded." The sheriff marked a line in the air with his finger. "Whatever the truth is lies somewhere between the extremes. We dig it out. We'll have our fill of digging before this is over."

Sam sighed and tossed the pencil into a scattering of papers. "While we keep one hand free to fight off the good citizens, eh? . . . But what's your personal opinion? Are they guilty?"

McKeogh shuffled together the loose papers, tapped these on edge to square them and laid them down. "I'd say the story Gutierrez and Morales told us makes sense enough. For now, consider that an unofficial statement."

Sam frowned. Vicente and Paco had insisted that they'd agreed earlier that at the first opportunity Paco would steal a jug of wine, steal off to meet Vicente, and the two would find a private place to drink it up. A logical place had been a lonely yard in back of two stores locked up for the night. They hadn't expected to find the body of a girl there, and the finding had half-paralyzed them. Should they report it to the sheriff or get away, as far and fast as possible? Suppose someone saw them before they got far? While they were debating the matter, the Flecher girl had come on the scene and screamed half the town onto their necks.

"But they ran like scared rabbits," Sam pointed out.

"If," McKeogh said slowly, "you were a Mexican who discovered the body of a raped and murdered white girl, and another white girl surprised you — what would you do?"

"Run," Sam answered wryly.

"Damn well told you would — for your life."

"Still, that's not saying why you think they didn't do it."

"How well you know Vicente Gutierrez?"

Sam's mouth tightened — remembering. He wasn't sure by a long shot that Rosa Morales hadn't lied about her cousin Vicente's whereabouts the night that his wife and Paddy Delaney were wantonly murdered. He caught McKeogh's steady eye then and flushed a little. He answered honestly: "Can't say I really do, Whit."

"Neither do I. The boy and his sister are alike in that way — morose, drawn into themselves, hard to know. But Paco — hell, everyone knows him. Shiftless, a liar, a petty thief. And also cheerful, never mad at a thing, friendly as a pup, tears in his eyes if he sees a fly with a crushed wing. Ethically, Paco is a crooked bum. By instinct — well, if everyone were like Paco Morales, you and I would go out of business." McKeogh paused weightily. "Sam — Paco didn't do this thing. He couldn't. And that means neither did Vicente, because after a thing like that, shaken like he was, Paco couldn't lie to protect anyone."

Sam nodded dourly. "He was crying like a baby when I locked 'em up."

McKeogh impatiently lifted his watch from a vest pocket. "What the hell is keeping Fletcher?"

Sam shrugged, thinking with distaste of Elkhorn's straitlaced banker. R.B. Fletcher had appeared on the scene as Dr. Enright, who served as coroner, was examining the murdered girl within minutes after the two lawmen had dispersed the mob. Sam remembered Enright's words as he and McKeogh had crouched there in the bare little lantern-lit yard. . . .

"Large contusion at the base of the skull. If you're open to hypothetical conjecture, Whit, I'd say the attacker was waiting in the alley mouth as Susie passed. Knocked her unconscious from behind and dragged her back here. Assaulted her — then strangled her. It's possible she never knew what happened after she was struck down. If so, it was God's own mercy. But it seems more likely that in fact she did revive for a moment — long enough to see his face. That's why he — or they — had to kill her."

McKeogh had agreed that this sounded likely, and then: "Doc, what's this raw line on her neck? Flesh is abraded and lacerated, like he used a rope, or wire. . . ."

"No. The strangling was done with his hands; I'll swear to that." Enright had paused. "More likely, she was wearing something, a necklace or locket, and he tore it off. Tore and yanked till it broke."

"Why," McKeough had mused, "if he wanted it, didn't he slip it off? or undo the catch?"

"Whit, the man was a maniac — had to be. Don't ask the whys!"

"Just pitching pennies, Doc. What I'm driving at, if he wanted some ornament because it was valuable, why break it? If he ripped it off in a frenzy, he had another reason. To him a powerful one."

Enright had shaken his head, a weary and negative gesture. "Whit, I just don't know. . . ."

Then R.B. Fletcher had made his appearance. He'd just escorted his daughter home, then had returned. Under the circumstances

Fletcher's usual stodgy, formal manner was ludicrous. He had cleared his throat and coldly suggested that when McKeogh had finished here, he wished to speak to him privately. Curtly the sheriff had told him to be at the office in a half-hour.

"Wish to hell he'd hurry," McKeogh grumbled now, tucking away his watch. "I want to get to bed."

"Fletcher said privately," Sam observed. "Maybe I better —"

"No," McKeogh said flatly. "You stay, Sam. Keeping me waiting is that ice-blooded bastard's little revenge for what he considers my improper conduct as a public official. I pamper the scum and ne'er-do-wells like Paco Morales, reason with them instead of clapping them behind bars for six months — for an occasional theft adding up to a couple of dollars per annum, for God's sake. Fletcher, you know, would like to demand a hundred per cent interest on a short term note. Then . . . he hasn't forgiven me for hiring you."

"Can't exactly blame him there," Sam observed wryly.

"You did make a palsied public spectacle of yourself for going on three months," McKeogh agreed, smiling. "The hell with him. Still, if you'd rather not. . . ."

"Why not, if he doesn't like it."

"Good. He couldn't hate me more'n he does —" The sheriff broke off as brisk steps sounded on the sidewalk beyond the open door, and R.B. Fletcher and his daughter entered.

The town banker was not a tall man, almost fleshless in the carefully tailored drape of his black broadcloth suit. His precise manner and speech contained an icy reserve. Mary Fletcher was a big, handsome, blonde girl of sixteen — physically like her fussy, nervous, lightheaded mother, temperamentally like neither parent. She gave both lawmen the full, gliding impact of her bold blue eyes — no more, because her father was watching. Apparently she'd effected an amazingly speedy recovery from her shocked hysteria of an hour ago.

"My daughter," Fletcher said stiffly, his arm circling her shoulders with protective pride, "says that she feels quite well enough to identify the pair and make a statement tonight. As this has been a dreadful experience for her, I thought it best not to prolong matters till tomorrow. I hope you'll oblige me, McKeogh."

The sheriff nodded. "This way, Mary." He lifted his key ring from a wall peg and unlocked the cellblock door. All of them entered, Sam bringing up the rear behind R.B. Fletcher.

The Mexican pair occupied a middle cell. Vicente lay on one wooden bunk, his arms folded behind his head, and he did not leave off his black study of the ceiling. Paco Morales huddled by the cell door, gripping the bars and weeping softly. He looked at them with pathetic eagerness. "Senor Whit," he whispered. "*Por Dios . . .* por Dios."

"Sorry, Paco," McKeogh said gently. "Well, Mary?"

She nodded very slowly, with wide-eyed candor. "Oh, yes. Yes. Those are the two, Mr. McKeogh."

"All right. Now tell me exactly what you saw — all of it from the beginning."

As she talked, McKeogh interrupted now and again, trying to shake her certainty on details. Each time she replied firmly, and Sam was convinced that her story was entirely straight.

"If that is all, sheriff, I'd like to speak to you privately a moment," Flether said coldly.

McKeogh motioned toward the office.

"Very well. Mary, wait here — away from that cell, please." The banker's fish-eyed glance lumped Sam with the two Mexicans as he preceded McKeogh into the office.

The sheriff closed the big wooden cellblock door, but their voices carried faintly through.

". . . shameful, horrible thing. And where in God's name were you, McKeogh?"

"Not being God, I was sitting here in stark ignorance. Where were you, R. B.?"

"I had no part in that lynching attempt, if that's what you're inferring. That was a disgusting affair."

"Why hell," McKeogh said gravely, "I knew you wouldn't break a word in the rule book, R. B."

A furious pause followed this sarcasm. Then Fletcher coughed. "This Susan Wells. She was not — she was not a decent girl. However —"

"That so? And who the hell ——"

"Let me finish," Fletcher snapped. "To answer your objection first — the girl's father is the town drunk. One of the town drunks," he amended loudly for Sam Ashby's ears.

Sam was studying the floor, and now he glanced at Mary Fletcher. She was leaning against the wall with her head tilted back and her face full of restless indifference. At once, meeting Sam's gaze, she smiled lazily and slightly arched her back. Her look then was entirely female and faintly predatory.

Papa Fletcher, if you only knew, Sam thought sardonically. Your little girl is missing her real call in life to beat all hell.

"R. B.," McKeogh was saying softly, "you're a small-souled mealy-mouthed hypocrite, but I'm too damned tired and out of sorts to ride herd on all your innuendoes. Get to the point."

The banker's voice was wintry and trembling. "The point is this: my daughter is of an age with that — that girl. Suppose that she had passed that alley before Susan Wells? As a father and a citizen, I speak for this community: your inexcusable negligence is to blame —"

"Paco! Paco, *cuidado!*" an urgent warning cry broke from Vicente Gutierrez. Sam spun on his heel and reached the cell in a couple of long strides. Paco was huddled on the floor, babbling a compulsive recitation of his many venial sins. Vicente was on his feet, his bony fists knotted at his sides and his lip curled faintly. In Spanish he spoke sardonically to Paco, to the effect that there was no priest here.

"What is it?" Sam asked harshly.

Vicente's dark eyes regarded him a fathomless moment. "A gun barrel. I see it stick between the bars of the window at Paco's back. When I shout, it pulled out. The man is gone." Again his lip curled. "But for how long, eh? You gringos cannot wait, it seems, to see the nooses on our necks."

The interior of the little adobe was a testimonial to scrupulous housecleaning. The packed clay floor had been so often swept that it was uneven with dips and hollows. Celsa Gutierrez sat at the caustic-bleached table, tapping her fingers on the cotton tablecloth of Mexican drawn-work. Her aunt, Mama Gonzales, was preparing coffee on the brick hearth, while Mama's daughter, Rosa, huddled in a chair close to Celsa, quietly sobbing and fingering her wooden rosary.

Celsa stirred restlessly, finally reaching in the pocket of her old duck jacket and taking out tobacco and papers. She rolled a cigarette, snapped a match aflame on her thumbnail and lighted her cigarette, her face pinched against the smoke. She did not like its acrid sting on her tongue and throat, and she smoked only when her moods of angry defiance reached a peak.

Rosa stopped weeping long enough to give Celsa, a long, reproachful glance. Rosa was a plump, pretty girl, obviously, even in her loose cotton nightgown, heavy with child — herself hardly more than a child. Now she resumed her sniffling.

Celsa squinted irritably through the smoke. "Does that help Paco? Por Dios, be patient."

Rosa's answer was a tremulous wailing sound.

Mama Gonzales turned from the hearth, the fat of her bulk trembling. Her round face was very grave. "I hope that we are doing the right thing in God's eyes, for Father Francisco will surely make us do penance when he learns of it."

"Do you think that Paco and Vicente are guilty, *tia?*" Celsa's query was sharp.

"That, no." Mama Gonzales sighed. "He is no good and a little crazy, that worthless son-in-law of mine, but this wicked thing — no. And Vicente is a good boy, though I do not understand him, nor you, Celsa *mia,*" she added severely. "You do not visit us often. And I don't see why you must go to live among gringos."

Celsa shrugged and blew smoke at the table-centered lamp. "I work among gringos. I like to eat anyway twice a day."

"I do not see why you don't marry a nice *nino* here. He would take care of you." Mama sniffed and turned back to the hearth. "How do you plan to set Paco and Vicente free?"

"That you will learn when El Pajarraco returns with Emiliano."

Celsa had left work early that day and gone home. She had been in bed when Ma Jagger had come to her shack, rousing her out, to tell her of the rape-murder, the attempted lynching of her brother and Paco Morales and their subsequent arrest and jailing. Celsa had wasted no time in hiring a livery horse and riding it hard all the way to Mextown. She had coldly known, even before Ma Jagger had finished her explanation, exactly what she was going to do. American law was for Americanos, not for Mexicans. Even the fair-minded *sereno* McKeogh, whom she liked and admired — though she would rather cut out her tongue than admit it, could not save Vicente or Paco from his fellow gringos who would fill the jurybox in an American court. They were already as good as condemned . . . unless. But she needed help, and she would find it only among her own people.

Withered little El Pajarraco, the husband of Mama Gonzales, now came breathlessly through the door. "I roused out Emiliano, Celsa. He will be here when he is dressed." El Pajarraco went promptly to a cupboard and took out a stone jug of *aguardiente.* The Ugly Bird turned it solemnly in his palsied hands, took a long pull, muttered, "Damnation to all *ladrones,*" and drank again.

Emiliano Morales, Paco's older brother, entered then like a gust of wind. He stole up behind Mama Gonzales and clamped a playful bear hug on her. *Maldiciones!* Great oaf!" Mama scolded and twisted around to rap him across the head with a ladle.

Emiliano whooped with delight and came over to the table. He was a hulking young man, a hard worker with a steadier temperament than Paco, yet more boisterous and extremely thickheaded. He moved between the two girls and dropped a large friendly arm over each of their shoulders, sliding his hands slyly to their breasts. Rosa pulled away and got to her feet, bursting into tears again as though this were the last straw.

Celsa slapped his hand away irritably. "Go on, Emiliano, sit down."

He fell into Rosa's chair facing Celsa, beaming hugely and patted her knee. She stamped on his foot. "Be serious, now. You know that Paco is in the *carcel?*"

"Oh, Paco is always in the carcel. Tonight he is in, tomorrow he is out. *A mi que?*"

"This is different," Celsa began patiently, then paused. The all-over situation was too complex. She could hammer it into Emiliano's brain by sheer repetition, but there

115

wasn't time. Emiliano could reason barely, and, at that, to not more than a day ahead. But offer him something that would require only action — ah, that was different. Once he'd grasped the fundamentals, Emiliano could handle any workaday job — or prank — better than most men because he was never diverted by his own thoughts.

She handed him her cigarette and Emiliano, pleased, took a deep drag, screwing his face up comically. Celsa smiled. "You are still driving a freight wagon for the lumber company of Lem Billings, eh, Emiliano?"

Emiliano nodded, squinting at her with ruttish slyness and pursing his lips around the cigarette.

"And you own your own wagon and mules? They are here in Mextown?"

"Where else, my little *enchilada?*"

Celsa winked at him. "How would you like to play a fine joke on the two men of law, McKeogh and Ashby? We can have some great fun with them."

Emiliano hooted. "I would rather have it with you, Celsa."

"I know, hombre; but do this thing for me, eh? I will come along."

"That is different. We will have good fun, eh, Celsa?"

■ ■ ■ ■

While Emiliano hitched up his team, Celsa argued the Gonzales' neighbors into the loan of a couple of horses. She and Emiliano rode to Elkhorn at a leisurely pace. As she'd hoped, by the late hour they'd arrived, every building on Jackson Street with the exception of the livery stable, was dark. After instructing the hulking one to circle wide on the flats behind the town, Celsa rode in alone and returned her livery horse to the stable. Then she hurried to the courthouse and joined Emiliano.

After cautioning him to be as silent as possible, she untied the two borrowed horses from the tailgate of the wagon and led them to the rear of the courthouse, ground-hitched them in readiness. When she returned, Emiliano maneuvered his wagon into position, backing it to within a few yards of the wall.

Moving close to that wall, Celsa spoke Vicente's name twice in a low hiss. Recognizing her voice, he pressed his face eagerly to a cell window.

"Celsa —"

"Do not talk. Only listen. In a moment you will find yourselves free, you and Paco.

I'll be waiting behind the building with two horses. Waste no time getting there. Do you understand?"

"Yes — yes."

At Celsa's sharp word, Emiliano swung off his seat and dropped into the wagon bed. He climbed out with a heavy length of logging chain, used to lash loads, slung from his shoulder. Following her directions he climbed onto the box and passed an end of the chain all around all six bars of the cell window and inserted the hook into a link. Next Emiliano secured the other end of the chain to the rear axle of his wagon by the main brace. All the while he was gurgling with suppressed glee, and Celsa had to bite her tongue to keep from fiercely hushing him; she didn't want to put him in a child-ish sulk at this crucial moment. The court-house was located at the end of town, and there was little likelihood of immediate discovery, but she kept casting nervous glances at the deserted street.

Emiliano mounted his seat again and took up his whip. His three-team mule hitch was, with its big sleek fellows — strong and well-cared for, the apple of Emiliano's eye. Softly he began to curse them, naming them many tender epithets. The six mules pricked up their ears eagerly, dancing into the feel of their collars. They surged into motion as he suddenly cracked his whip . . . straining against the braked weight. Then Emiliano threw off the brake.

The wagon shot forward and the logging chain lifted and sang taut. A small prayer choked in Celsa's throat as the rear wheels lifted clear of the ground — hung suspended for a split second. Then with a crash and tear of splintering wood, the window frame tore free, ripping strips of sheathing and siding from both flanks. The debris leaped outward and crashed into the dust, and then the frame collapsed and the bars slipped out, freeing the logging chain which bounded Emiliano's wagon as he whipped his team away across the flats toward the Mextown road, shouting his delight at the stars.

Celsa lingered long enough to see her brother begin his climb through the gaping hole, and then she hurried back to the horses and held them ready as Vicente and Paco ran up. They snatched their reins and leaped into saddle.

"Listen," Celsa said swiftly, fiercely. "Head for that old caved-in soddy fifteen miles to the north of Tie Creek. You know the place, Vicente — stay there. I'll come tomorrow with food. When you're safely across the creek, turn the horses loose — they'll return to Mextown. And Vicente, there is a pistol and bullets in your saddlebag. Now ride hard!"

Paco needed no second urging; he drummed his heel against his mount's flanks and streaked away across the moonlit flats. Vicente hesitated, holding in his prancing animal. His voice was choked with emotion. *"Hermana mia —"*

"Go on!" She almost screamed it, and then Vicente wheeled and headed after Paco.

Celsa watched his going for only a moment; she turned and ran with long, lithe strides along the rear of the buildings toward South Jackson. She had nearly reached her shanty when the first faint sounds of aroused townsfolk drifted to her ears. Only then, hidden by the lonely darkness, did she permit herself a bitter smile.

CHAPTER EIGHT

Aroused by the jailbreak, both Sam and the sheriff were on the scene within minutes. For the second time that night they found themselves studying the ground beneath the cell window by lantern-light.

Earlier, when they had searched for signs after the attempt on Paco's life, they'd found only a few indistinct, scuffed boot-marks hopelessly blurred in the soft ground. Whoever it was had stood on a box to lift himself eye-level to the window. If Vicente, lying face-up on the bunk beneath, hadn't seen the gun-barrel nose above the sill and shouted a warning, Paco would have taken a point-blank bullet in the back. The alarm had broken the would-be assassin's nerve; he'd disappeared when Sam Ashby and McKeogh had reached the spot.

R.B. Fletcher was enough shaken by the incident to call off his haranguing of the sheriff; he'd ushered his daughter out the door, pausing long enough to say vindictively that McKeogh hadn't heard the last of this. The sheriff had snuffed the lamp affixed to the corridor wall, leaving the cell-block in darkness. "They'll be safe enough if nobody can see inside to shoot," he'd told Sam as he locked up the office. "Let's get some shut-eye."

Then, within the hour, the break-out had brought them on the run from their hotel rooms. McKeogh had been aroused from a sound sleep by the night hostler from the livery stable, who'd been the first to ascertain what had happened. At first they were mystified by the ragged gap in the cell wall, as though a giant fist had smashed through, flinging a shambles of boards and frame and iron bars a dozen paces away. Then McKeogh, tracing the soft ground with a low-held lantern, delved the truth. "It took something with a lot of momentum and weight to do the job, and here's your answer — a heavy wagon with two, three teams." The feeble lantern-glow picked out sharp-sunk wheel ruts and hoof-marks.

"Here's some sorry footprints," Sam pointed out, adding dourly: "They don't tell much."

"Enough maybe," McKeogh said softly. "One set belongs to a woman. Here . . . see the small narrow sole, the sharp heel?" His finger traced the rough outline of a fairly clear track.

Both men straightened, eyes meeting with a common thought. Sam took a deep angry breath, slowly let it out. "She should have thought she'd be the first suspect, the natural one."

"She likely did," the sheriff said curtly. "And just as likely she didn't give a damn. She thinks an almighty lot of that brother, more than he's worth, maybe. Not for us to judge. . . . She had help, that's sure. From Mextown, of course. And that thick-skulled brother of Paco's owns a big freighter that would have done the job nicely."

"Really takes the bit in her teeth, don't she?" Sam said thinly.

The sheriff met his hot stare mildly. "Uh-huh. Got gall a-plenty, that girl. Makes your blood boil, eh?"

"Well, why the hell. . . ." Sam broke off, feeling a deep flush burn slowly from his collar. He saw McKeogh's point perfectly: a few months ago, Sam Ashby had been a man to bull ahead by himself, forging out his selfish destiny without regard for the rights of others or for the general good. The man's last major act had been to throw Vicente Gutierrez off his homestead, and he'd since realized how that act had ruthlessly broken something in young Gutierrez' fine-tempered spirit — a sense of personal dignity that Vicente must have fought to achieve. If tonight Celsa Gutierrez had acted with the same headstrong blindness, her action was at least prompted by fierce loyalty to a brother whose life was at stake.

"All right," he murmured. "I get, Whit."

"I know that," McKeogh said shortly. "Now let it go until morning. Not much we can do till it's light, and you'll need all the sleep you can get. Unless I'm mistaken, you'll have a long day, a long trail ahead. . . ."

When first true dawn bled down the east ramparts of the Elks, the two men left the hotel and tramped across town to Celsa Gutierrez' shanty. At this hour the town lay silent as the early sunrays struck a mellow softening along the starkly false-fronted buildings of Jackson Street. Still free of dust and heat, the air was cool and windless. McKeogh mechanically took out his old pipe, then tucked it away with a shake of his head.

"Air's too fine to spoil with a smoke." He sniffed appreciatively. "Been a spell since

I've been up with the sun. Best time of the day . . . a thing the young forget too soon and the old remember too late."

Sam's long, somber face was scowl-set with thought. "Whit . . . if we bring those boys back, what chance will they stand in a court of law?"

McKeogh was silent a time, slowing his stiff strides. "There's the Fletcher girl," he said slowly. "She'll be testifying for the prosecution, and her testimony will be solid. That girl is anything but flighty or empty-headed." He smiled a little. "Her trouble is otherwise."

Sam gave a wry grunt of assent.

"So if we find anything that helps 'em," McKeogh added, "it won't be through shaking Mary Fletcher's story. She told it straight, of that I'm sure. All right, someone, a lone man, tried to kill Paco last night. Let's juggle that hot potato . . . tell me why."

Sam shrugged. "Anybody in the lynch mob could have made the try."

"Could have. But did they?" A mob, McKeogh mused aloud, acts in concert to the mob's will, without a personal sense of moral responsibility. An unwritten law of society recognizes this, and so a mob is not held liable for its acts. But suppose that a single member of that mob commits an identical act. Then — barring insanity — he is a cold-blooded murderer who has violated man's strongest moral law, an act on which mankind in all times and places has laid the harshest taboos. Every mother's son is ingrained with that moral restraint, or society would fly to pieces. Every man in last night's mob, with time to think coolly, would realize that the law would mete proper punishment. Was there, McKeogh concluded, a man in that mob that Sam would care to put his finger on and say, this is a murderer?

The deputy shook his head, doubtfully, for he still followed with difficulty the logical abstractions of which McKeogh was so fond. "Well, then?"

"Two possibilities," said McKeogh. "Our would-be-killer of Paco was crazy, a fanatical reformer of some sort, or he had a powerful motive that might or might not have had anything to do with the rape-killing. . . . Well, here we are."

They'd crossed the railroad tracks and a cinder apron and clambered down an enbankment into a track-side dip where Celsa Gutierrez lived. Sam hadn't taken real note of the place before, and now he saw that Celsa had made this rundown shanty more than livable. Several coats of whitewash, new shakes on the roof, a patch of lawn and a cinder path testified to a proud home-maker.

McKeogh rapped lightly at the door. Celsa opened it almost at once. She wore the gray wrapper that Sam remembered and held a cigarette between her fingers. Her expression was one of flinty defiance.

"Buenos dias, Celsa. Usual question — may I come in?"

"Pretty quick your gringo frien's will start to talk, sheriff," she said coldly, moving aside. McKeogh chuckled as he entered, removing his hat, and Sam followed suit. The interior of the single room was very clean and tidy.

Turning to face her, McKeogh chided mildly, "Now do I ever trouble you without a reason?"

She shrugged, drawing on the cigarette and letting smoke trickle from her nostrils. "I don' read your thoughts."

"You read them this time, Celsa. Was it Emiliano who helped you break Paco and Vicente out last night?"

Celsa Gutierrez picked a fleck of tobacco from her lower lip and studied it. "Did someone break them out?"

"You shouldn't have left tracks all over the place. Dead giveaway."

"Were there tracks, sheriff?" she inquired, arching an eyebrow mockingly. "You can show they are mine, yes? The law, they tell me, needs a lot of proof. But I forget — not where greasers are concerned."

McKeogh said flatly, sharply, "You know me better than that, Celsa."

The girl's angry stare faltered, and Sam thought for a moment she would apologize. But not Celsa Gutierrez; again he glimpsed the hard, fierce pride of her in the sharp backtilt of her head. "I say again — you know these footprints, they are mine?"

"A small bluff," McKeogh said wearily. "They could have belonged to most women. But you're bluffing, too, Celsa. I want to know where Paco and Vicente are. You know if anyone does. Out with it."

There was sudden fire in her snapping black eyes. "And if I know, you think I tell you? You're crazy, mister. After what happen las' night —"

"What happened last night, we stopped," McKeogh cut in sharply. "Ashby and me. Or didn't you hear that?"

The corners of her mouth drooped sullenly. "I hear. But you listen — !"

"No, you listen. What you don't know is that someone tried to shoot Paco later. Your brother spotted a gun muzzle in the window or Paco would be a dead man. Not one of that mob; I think some loner had a reason for wanting to see Paco, maybe Vicente, too, dead before the hangman had a chance. Can you tell me anything about that?"

There was a break of fear in Celsa's mask now; she moistened her lips, shook her head negatively. "What — what did Vicente and Paco say?"

"Told me they hadn't a notion who might want to see either of 'em dead that bad. If they were lying, I couldn't tell. . . . Now you see why I've got to find those two boys? When news of the break gets around, that someone'll be looking for them. If he finds them before we do — dammit, girl, don't you see all you've done is make 'em free game in an open field?"

"If they leave the basin —" Unconsciously she spoke her first thought aloud, quickly broke off.

"It won't help," McKeogh said gently. "If they get out of the basin, all they can hope for is to hide and be hunted till they're captured or shot. That kind of hide-and-seek is a killing game; I don't think either of them have the stomach for it. If they stay here, we — or the other one — will find them. Best chance they got is safely locked in my jail. I'll take every precaution possible to keep them alive till the trial."

"But — then?" Celsa's lips barely moved.

McKeogh shook his head. "I can only tell you this — I'll try like hell to find the real killer of that girl."

"You don't believe — ?"

"I think they're innocent. You know I'm not bluffing now."

She gave a bare nod.

"Then, as you say, there's no proof you broke 'em out. Could be Vicente visited you last night after the break — told you where he and Paco were going?"

"That maybe happen," Celsa conceded stonily.

"And what did he tell you?"

She didn't reply for a moment; then: "If I say — what happens?"

"I send Ashby to bring 'em in. You ride along — try to persuade them to give up quietly. I only hope you can." McKeogh sighed profoundly. "They wouldn't be armed, by pure chance?"

Celsa bit her lip. "They have a pistola." Her fierce stare swung to Sam Ashby. "Yes, I go along. And you will take Vicente alive and well. If you hurt him, gringo — I kill you, I swear it!"

"That's a bargain," Sam said coldly.

CHAPTER NINE

As Sam emerged from the livery stable leading two horses, Celsa came up with a bulky flour sack swinging from her hand. She was dressed as she'd been the first time he had seen her — in a full dark skirt and a man's jacket. It had occurred to Sam, after he'd told the hostler to ready a pair of mounts, to add that a sidesaddle be cinched on one. Celsa had ridden astride, as a squaw might, on that other occasion, but now there was no call for haste. She was sensitive in her way, and no fool; she might interpret a man's saddle as a slur at her Indian blood. Though at the moment he felt deep resentment for her antagonizing manner, Sam had no wish to strike back that way. If he also had a faint desire for her good opinion, he flatly self-denied as much.

Celsa halted, glancing at the sidesaddle and then at him, her dark face expressionless. Her voice was cold though not hostile.

"I bring some sandwiches and coffee."

Sam merely nodded, took the flour sack and knotted it to his saddle horn, then helped her mount. Her arm was stiff against his hand. Afterward he stepped into his saddle, ranged alongside her.

"Mind mentioning now where we're going?"

"There is an old soddy north of Tie Creek in a little valley. . . ."

"The old Murchison place?"

"Yes."

Sam grunted and put his horse into motion. She had chosen an ideal place for the fugitives to lie low — for he was sure that Celsa had herself selected their hideaway. He still had a lingering doubt about the propriety of the sheriff's overlooking her part in the break-out which she'd doubtless engineered entirely. The sheriff had all but assured her that he'd let the matter drop quietly from sight. No small offense, though Sam had seen McKeogh bend the letter of the law to distortion before this, always with good reason. Aside from his doubts as an officer, Sam did feel a hint of pleasure at the sheriff's decision, but at the same time it obscurely angered him.

He held bleak silence as they rode steadily through the morning, holding a northeasterly route till they hit the sluggish flow of Tie Creek. Now they followed the creek upstream, holding off from its bank choked by dense willow thickets, hung with whining hordes of mosquitoes. A couple of miles farther the creek greatly widened, laced by pale sandbars. They splashed across the shallows and soon reached the sand and clay hills of the north basin. The rich grass flats petered out, and the land heightened. The hills were slashed by ravines, bisected by steep washes. Here was grass, but it was sparse and poor, and the ground was baked hard, almost impervious to a plowblade, shrunk and sun-dried with deep cracks clogged by dead grass and burrs. The sun was strong and merciless as they headed into it.

While the hot forenoon held, they covered another five miles of rough country, and then Sam said, "We'll eat now."

They dismounted on a stony rise, and Sam ground-tied the horses, took down the flour sack and handed it to Celsa. She seated herself on a rock, and Sam hunkered down a few paces away. She lifted out an earthenware jug, pulled the cork with her teeth and filled a tin cup. Sam accepted it with a nod of thanks, and she filled one for herself, took out a sandwich, set the sack on the ground between them and swung sideways to ignore him while she ate in silence.

Sam bit into a beef sandwich without much relish, sipped the lukewarm coffee. He faced deliberately away from the girl, but presently found his glance drawn back to her. Celsa ate slowly but with a healthy appetite in spite of her deep worry for Vicente. Approving of her good sense, he studied her covertly. She had removed her jacket against the heat and she sat erect, the lithe, rangy strength of her tall body not concealed by the frayed shabbiness of her skirt and prim cotton blouse of wash-faded pink. Her head was well shaped on her smooth brown neck, the black shining hair cropped off sensibly below her collar and drawn tight at the back of her neck by a limp blue ribbon. She had pushed her tattered straw hat back, and Sam could see her forehead was finely beaded with perspiration.

Curiously Sam eyed her profile, wondering if he should revise his first impression . . . no, even in this pose, she simply was not attractive. Her eyebrows were too heavy, ruled almost pencil-straight above her piercing eyes; her nose was too long and thin, her mouth too wide. Yet most Mexican girls, while uncommonly pretty in their teens, went early to a slovenly fading, the lot of all frontierswomen, and he had the impression that Celsa Gutierrez would still be a firmly trim and damnably striking woman when she was fifty. Striking . . . that was the word, and particularly now, with her sharp features softened by a pensive concentration as he looked across the brown rolling land to a gray-black horizon jutting against the far sky. Primitive people, Indians especially, had that ability — to sink unknowing into their surroundings, every sense alert and yet divorced from time and space — and Sam knew a brief envy.

Suddenly Celsa swung her head, her black stare full on his. "Well," she said roughly, "you had enough?" She motioned toward the foot sack, but Sam's neck felt warm anyway. He nodded yes and got quickly to his feet, moving to the horses.

The land got progressively rougher, ranging northward, and they picked their way slowly, swinging circuitously around small gorges too deep to negotiate. Twice they stopped to rest the horses. Finally, as they ascended from a steep dip, a long rugged ridge grew along the skyline, and this marked the south end of the little valley where old Deaf Murchison had erected his little soddy.

It seemed unlikely that anyone had ever purposely made a home here — the most isolated and desolate spot of all — in this unfriendly northern part of Two Troughs Basin. But old Deaf, Sam recalled, had been an unfriendly and desolate man, a recluse who'd prospected a sprinkling of gold pockets whose location he'd kept a jealously guarded secret. Not that they'd yielded enough to tempt anyone's greed, for Deaf had grubbed enough dust only to buy bare necessities on his rare visits to Buckhorn; for the rest, he'd lived off the land. Once when he'd failed to show up in town for six months, a couple of citizens had ridden out to his soddy. Evidently the old man had died in his sleep, his bones long since picked clean.

It was a sober reminder to Sam of the lonesomeness of this shunned place where Whit McKeogh had dispatched him to handle a real job on his own; with this, he had a grim resolve not to fail the sheriff's trust. He hoped that neither fugitive would offer resistance, or he'd have to divide a wary attention between them and the girl. He wondered worriedly if she had a gun concealed somewhere. . . . One bridge at a time, he thought coldly.

Celsa broke his thoughts abruptly: "Why

don' the sheriff come along?"

"He got piled up by a bronc a while back . . . hurt him inside. He can't ride much."

She gave him a long careful regard, seemed about to speak again, and Sam wondered if she'd remind him of her earlier threat, but she only looked away and off toward the ridge, her gaze restless now and worried. They started up the gradual ascent with Sam taking the lead.

Halfway to the summit of the ridge, a bullet whirred past Sam's chest.

It was off by a good foot but seared across his horse's neck, sending the animal careening in a panic as the clear report of the rifle lashed echoes across the stony height. The horse got into the feel of its savage gyrations and commenced bucking furiously. Sam held the saddle a stubborn moment, thought better of it then and flung himself sideways and outward.

The raw ground tilted wildly to meet him and he tried to light on his shoulder and side, but only partly succeeded. With his mouth full of dirt and body numbed by the jolting impact, Sam rolled blindly from the flailing hoofs. He scrambled behind the nearest shelter, a low flat boulder; Celsa half fell out of her saddle and flung herself breathlessly down at his side. Sam's horse raced downslope with a perky show of heels, and Celsa's trotted after it.

A second slug screamed off the rock. Sam quickly raised his head to peer above it, scanning the upper ridge to his far right. He caught a confused glimpse of pale powdersmoke smudging a clump of brush at the crest before he ducked back. That entire section of the ridge was choked with a heavy growth of elderberry brush . . . damned fine cover for the ambusher. And maybe me, Sam thought, if I can get closer. It was a good piece to the summit, and the unseen rifleman hadn't laid his sights properly to allow for downhill shooting, always a tricky business. Or I'd be a dead man . . . may still be.

With that thought, he glanced quickly at Celsa, crowded against him and breathing audibly through her clenched teeth. "You say your brother only had a pistol?"

Her eyes glared hotly into his, inches away. "You think he shoot when I am with you?"

"You know him better'n me."

"Vicente would not do this! And 'ow can he know we are coming?"

Sam shifted his hip to ease its pressure against a jagged abutment of the boulder, considering. Poor chickenhearted Paco would not shoot to save his life, and if not Vicente — then who?

Someone who had hung unseen on the trail of Celsa and himself, who'd judged their destination and cut around at a furious pace to get ahead of them and wait on the ridge. If he was the same party who'd been scared off last night, he must have hung around, keeping his ears open. Learning of the jail break, he'd guessed there would be a pursuit of the fugitives — had simply followed Sam and Celsa. This remote, lonely spot was prime for a killer to finish his work — and I've led him here, Sam thought disgustedly.

But if that's so, why'd he wait to take a pot shot at you? How do you know it's the same man? Sam's head ached with swarming possibilities; he gave it up. He bit his lip and surveyed the upslant of the ridge. Beyond the boulder lay a bare stretch, terminated by the deep cut of a dry wash which meandered sideways and upward till it was lost in the chokecherry brush. If he could reach the wash without being cut down in his tracks. . . . The two shots had been wide-spaced. A single-shot rifle with its delay in breeching a load would make the first part easy enough . . . draw his fire, then run like hell.

Again Sam raised his head, exposing his hat and eyes. He saw the faint stir of foliage at the spot his eyes marked high above, and at once he flattened down again. He felt Celsa move against him, lifting on her elbows to follow the direction of his glance. With straining haste he clamped a big hand between her shoulders and forced her hard against the earth, snarling, "Get it down!"

Celsa twisted her head and spat dirt and an angry epithet lost in the roar of the rifle. The slug gouged the ground a foot away, launching stinging sand against their faces. Celsa gave a startled little yelp as Sam reared up, drawing his knees beneath him and driving to his feet in the same motion, lunging forward almost before he had his footing. His long legs piledrove him in a leaning crouch for the arroyo fifteen feet away. Its sandly lip crumbled as it caught his weight and he skidded down the brief incline on his back, digging in his heels.

Hitting the gravel bottom, he rolled out flat on his belly with gun in hand. For an instant he had the sharp worry that Celsa might try to follow . . . as usual he'd acted without words, thinking first of himself he knew with guilty self-censure. A lifetime habit that died hard. Yet she'd evidently grasped his intent readily enough, remaining where she was. A good thing . . . for now the ambusher had reloaded; his next slug thudded high into the wash bank, cascading down gravel and sand against Sam's leg. He knew then that he was effectively cut off from the man's view.

He dug in his elbows and toes and began to move forward up the arroyo on his stomach. Alternately doubling each leg and straightening it, boot-thrusting at the loose gravel, and so achieving his goal by cautious inches. The rubble rasped along his chest and thighs and sweat broke on his brow and ran in a stinging wash into his eyes. He sleeved it away and moved on. The slope steepened steadily; it was a long way to the fringing brush, and the tortuous winding of the wash began to pinch down. He worked slowly upward for a quarter hour, and the rifleman did not shoot again.

When Sam reached the first thicket he was drenched with sweat and panting for breath . . . this Indian crawl was no kid's game. With infinite care, because the ambusher would have guessed his purpose by now, he ascended the bank on his hands and knees and slipped through a narrow opening in the brush, worked low-crouched on an upslope zigzag toward the rifleman's position, while holding to dense cover.

Still the man held fire. Sam's belly crawled with tension. Careful as he was, he knew the unknown couldn't fail to make out a stir of foliage as he slipped through it. His eyes raked the banked brush ahead and found no betraying movement. The man had only to patiently wait till Sam was close, then take a certain aim on his approach —

The bullet lashed like an angry hornet through space inches above his bent back — would have taken him high in the chest if he'd been erect. Sam dived for the ground, scrambled to his knees and fanned three shots swiftly at the line of fire. He flattened out again, his heart pounding against the earth — waited. No sound reached his straining ears. He got to his knees, feeling a bit foolish. That hasty, half-panicked reaction had accomplished nothing. Pistol-fanning couldn't score on a broad barn wall beyond a few yards, and obviously his adversary hadn't yet seen him, had fired at a telltale agitation of brush. One thing . . . he was near enough for the rifle to lend no edge against His Remington handgun.

He moved upward a single cautious step and halted, hearing the crackle of brush as the man broke at last, running left along the ridge crest. Sam fired at the sound and then started a running climb, furiously breasting the brush. He heard the abrupt tattoo of hoofs; the unknown had reached his horse, was in saddle and cutting on left across the ridgetop.

Cursing and perspiring, lashed by stinging branches, Sam wallowed through the last thicket . . . too late. The ambusher had vanished over a shoulder of ridge. Sam sighed and lowered his gun. He tramped over to where the man had lain in concealment. The spot where he had crouched behind a bush was plainly marked, and he'd cut away a small patch of twigs and leaves. Sam hunkered down and sighted through it, taking a clear view of the open slope far below. He saw the dark crown of Celsa's head lift cautiously above the boulder which still sheltered her.

About to stand erect and hail her, he thought better of it. He moved to the opposite flank of the summit and let his gaze travel the little valley below. It lay long and narrow between two high ridges; against the far ridge Deaf Murchison had built his soddy, gophering into the hillside and adding a foreroof of crisscross poles laid over by sod squares. Part of the roof had caved in, one corner post now jutting up forlornly. Rainwater sluicing down the hillside had melted most of the wall sodding back into the earth, so that little substantial remained of the dwelling except a few unrotted logs. The doorway was a square of inky shadow intensified by the glaring sunlight outside. A sagging windlass frame stood in the yard above a well-hole and to one side was a small truck garden overrun by weeds. The pole corral opposite was broken down and empty . . . Celsa had told Sheriff McKeogh that the boys would probably turn loose the horses on which they'd left Elkhorn; at least that avenue of escape was checked.

Sam drew and released an unsteady breath and started his descent to the valley floor. The ridge was brush free on this side, and the fugitives, alarmed by the shots, would probably be watching from within the soddy. Once he was inside pistol range, there was no way to effectively cover his approach. He hoped grimly that Vicente would not resist or attempt to break . . . but if he did, Sam was damned if he'd have Celsa at his back.

Celsa was well enough off where she was, ignorant of his intention. McKeogh might be displeased, and Celsa would surely hate him with a redoubled passion, even if he took Vicente and Paco unharmed. For a moment he hesitated, then the old unrelenting stubbornness dominated his thoughts. The hell with both of them; this was his job and he'd handle it his way.

He reached the flat valley-bottom and trudged slowly toward the soddy, his gun pointed before him. He kept the flimsy obstacle of the old windlass between himself and the soddy, fixing a steady concentration on the doorway till his vision grew spotty. There wasn't, apparently, a breath of life inside . . . excepting perhaps the rats. Had Vincente and Paco broken already, hearing the shots? If so, they hadn't gotten far afoot.

He halted beside the windlass, raising his voice sharply: "Gutierrez — Morales. Come out with your hands high . . . no gun."

The quavering chirp of Paco's voice issued from the darkness. "No shoot, Meester Sam . . . no shoot."

"Gutierrez?"

"Paco is alone, Meester Sam . . . no shoot."

The young Mexican's squat form emerged from the soddy. He moved with a spiritless shuffle, blinking against the hot brightness. Sam tramped over to him, and Paco's black quick eyes shifted wildly, to avoid the tall man's flinty stare.

Sam let his gun off-cock, saying harshly, "Where is he?"

Paco's hands fumbled against the chest of

his grubby cotton shirt. "Vicente, he took off pronto when shooting start. He is running that way." Paco pointed at a wide break in the ridgeside about thirty yards to the right of the soddy.

"You stay here, boy. Don't budge from this spot, *sabe?*"

Paco Morales gave a quick frightened nod, then blurted, "He have the gun, Meester Sam. It is big bluff, I think. You will not shoot — ?"

"Depends on him."

Sam was pivoting as he spoke, heading for the break at a fast trot. A faint cry drifted from the far slope, and he paused to glance around. Celsa was stumbling down from its summit, the dust furling about her running feet. She was still distant enough, Sam grimly noted, and ignored her then, swinging into the cleft.

The cleft penetrated clear through the ridge and beyond lay a field of jumbled stone. Sam swore and slowed his pace. A man might play hide-and-seek for hours in that monolithic maze of giant boulders. He pushed stubbornly on, plunging a labyrinthic route through, climbing the smaller rocks and skirting the larger.

. . . A bullet puffed dust from a rock surface well above his head and whined viciously off. Shot echoes clapped across the rock field. Sam saw Vicente's black head duck back from sight not many feet away. The boy had taken his stand behind a tremendous slab, and he'd deliberately fired high.

"Go back!" he shrilled in Spanish. "*Que te sirva de escarmiento,* gringo!"

Sam veered sideways to slip behind cover of a good-sized boulder. For a moment he scanned the cluttered upheaval of the field, roughed it out in his mind's eye, then sat down and tugged off his boots. Crouching his body small, he slid to an adjacent boulder, then to another, skirting in a wide circle to get behind Vicente unseen. His sock feet moved soundlessly over the rocks, and hastily, for each was red-hot. Otherwise it was simple; within a few minutes he stumbled into sight of the boy . . . so unexpectedly that he had to fade quickly back to shelter.

Vicente stood at the end of a sandy amphitheatre about three yards in diameter, his back to Sam. He was still intent on the spot he'd seen the deputy vanish, his pistol held ready.

Sam stooped and picked up a pebble, lobbing it high above Vicente's head; it struck out of sight off to the right with a smaller clatter. The boy spun instantly, firing wildly, again and yet again.

Skittish as a scared colt, Sam thought . . . knew if he covered Vicente and called on him to surrender, the boy would likely come around shooting. From this range he could bring the kid down by a bullet in the shoulder or leg with contemptuous ease . . . a good way to cripple a man for life. Kill or cripple, there's a fine choice.

There was one remaining choice, and having made it, Sam didn't let himself dwell on it. He tossed another pebble. This time Vicente held fire but stiffened to sharp attention as it struck, craning his neck — and now Sam left shelter, darting low and fast across the sandy clearing that separated them.

He was still two yards distant when the sound of his feet brought Vicente wheeling about, swinging his pistol in a tight arc. Sam dived the last few straining feet, slamming into the boy full-tilt. Vicente was driven solidly against the slab with a grunting explosion of breath.

Sam grabbed wildly at the gun to thrust it aside and then his driving feet slipped and he fell to his knees, trying to salvage the maneuver of grappling Vicente's legs with one arm, his other hand immobilizing the pistol barrel. The boy sought to push away from the rock where Sam's weight pinned him and could not. With a burst of panicked strength, he wrenched the gun from Sam's grasp, chopped it viciously up and down. The muzzle caught Sam across the temple, and to escape the pain he let go of Vicente and rolled away, his hand dipping for his gun.

He was on his knees and left hand as his right closed about the Remington butt — saw Vicente with his gun leveled now, yet hesitating — then Celsa's piercing cry froze them both as they were.

She ran the last few stumbling feet to the great slab and leaned against it, her head bent, sobbing for breath. Vicente pointed at Sam and rattled off something in Spanish.

Celsa's eyes flashed as she flung back her head, shaking it fiercely because she was too winded to talk. Vicente started an angry objection as Sam now climbed slowly to his feet, his gun drawn but dangling loosely at his side. He wisely said nothing as Celsa gasped out a furious order. Vicente did not move. Celsa repeated her words, at the same time catching him roughly by the arm and shoving him toward the valley opening. Her brother sullenly hunched his head between his shoulders and tramped away.

Celsa only now glanced at Sam; he braced himself for a tongue-lashing. Instead she said quietly, "He will wait with Paco. They will go back with us." There was a toneless finality to her words, and Sam felt a stab of shame. This with his puzzled surprise that a Mexican male of Gutierrez' spirit should so meekly obey his sister. In a flash it came to him how Celsa's protective domination of Vicente had become an ingrained habit that left the boy's self-respect sadly vulnerable. The kid had probably never seen any crisis through on his own; there had always been Celsa to fight out his fights.

Unbidden, Sam felt a wondering pity for them, this pair of defiant orphans, and it must have shown in his expression. Celsa stiffened erect, her lips tightening to a hard line. She took a step toward him and then her gaze widened; she cocked her head.

"You bleeding bad, gringo."

Sam became aware of the hot wetness cutting raggedly down his cheek and neck and seeping through his shirt. Vicente's blow had laid a shallow gash across his hairline; he touched it gingerly, shrugged. But Celsa had already swung away, lifting the hem of her dusty skirt and tearing off a strip of petticoat.

"Sit down," she said curtly.

Sam opened his mouth and closed it and then sank down on his haunches. The gentleness of her hands surprised him.

"I didn't figure —"

"Oh be still!"

CHAPTER TEN

"A couple dollars' worth, Mr. Bardeen," Boone MacLaughlin said. He discovered that his voice was trembling with anger, paused to steady it. "A couple lousy dollars' worth of grub. It won't break you." He ran a bitter eye over the goods-bulging shelves. "Not any, it won't."

Amos Bardeen's eyes were owlish and unblinking behind his thick spectacles. "Not a cent of credit. I'm sorry, young man. If you had collateral —"

"Collateral!" Boone spat. "You a damned banker or what?"

"A businessman, sir," Mr. Bardeen's reedy voice did not alter by a jot. "A businessman's business, like a bank's, is to make money. And you, Mr. MacLaughlin, are a bad risk."

"Well, dammit — !"

"You've noted, I believe, that there is a lady present." Mr. Bardeen gave a slight nod toward fat Mrs. Jourgenson who had just entered, darting her little eyes over some cloth bolts on a counter and studiously pretending not to hear a word. "I will not tolerate offensive language in this establishment. I suggest that you leave before I fetch the sheriff."

Boone stared at this thin and pompous little storekeeper whom he could have knocked spinning with a swing of his big calloused palm. But neither words nor violence could have expressed his raging disgust, and he turned suddenly and tramped from the general-goods store.

He stood on the plankwalk in the cool twilight, hands fisted tightly against the fevered wrath burning in him. Like his father's before him, his temper was swift to flare, quick to die. He had discovered long ago that if he could master the blind intensity of it for a few moments, he could beat it. But one of these days . . . !

His own savage vindictiveness sobered him at once. Get a cinch on that temper and keep it tight. Ain't it fetched you enough trouble?. . . .

Seven years ago Boone's father, a peppery man with more mulish determination than good sense, had bought a small ranch in Two Troughs Basin and promptly brought in a flock of sheep to stock it. The local cow-men were moved from unbelieving amusement at the feisty old fool's threat to stunned anger when he carried it out. Things happened . . . from mysterious snipers taking pot shots at the woolies to the MacLaughlin house being burned to the ground while old MacLaughlin and his eighteen-year-old son were absent. And the old man fought back tooth and nail. Shooting steers, firing warning shots at taunting cowboys, picking fights with them in town. Till one night he was shot and killed in a quarrel with a drunken cowhand, and the jury, without leaving the courtroom, brought in a unanimous verdict of self-defense.

Young Boone, without counting odds, had gone after the acquitted killer and called him out. Screamed some crazy challenge that now lay blurred in his memory, and when the killer went for his gun, Boone drew and shot him twice in the belly. The man had died a week later. There had been no witnesses to the encounter, and again the local jurymen passed a swift verdict. Young Boone MacLaughlin, swearing that the dead man had pulled his gun first, was sentenced to five to ten years in the state penitentiary.

In serving out those five long bleak years, Boone had learned how to master himself. Afterward he had returned to his father's small run-down ranch in Two Troughs Basin because it was all he had — carrying in him, at twenty-three, a lifetime burden of seething and bitter hatred for the world. He'd needed money, and only Sam Ashby, a hard but just cowman, had given him a chance. Ashby, who had not needed a third man on his little ranch crew, had hired Boone on for a year, and Boone had carefully saved every dollar of his meager pay to stock his sorry range with a few cattle. After two grueling years, during which Boone had lived on next to nothing, working from dawn to dark and stumbling into his blankets drugged with exhaustion, it had seemed he might turn a small profit. That was before part of his little herd got into a larkspur patch, swelled up and died.

Nothing to do but drive himself harder and hang on, somehow.

But a man had to eat. It had come to the point where he was subsisting on tubers and berries and jackrabbits for which he laid crude snares because shells for his battered old Colt cost money. But a man could only drive himself to a point and then he was standing on quicksand . . . something had to give. And Boone, in this moment of his failure to purchase a sorry two dollars' worth of salt and flour, knew a first dim fear that he was reaching that point.

He stood on the boardwalk, a gaunted young man in a ragged linsey-woolsey shirt and threadbare jeans, his fists balled tightly in his hip pockets. A bitter blackness in his stare that ranged across the town of Elkhorn, which he hated, with all it held in past and present repudiation of him. The sorriest drunk could obtain a few pennies' worth of credit — but not Boone Mac-Laughlin, the sheepman's son, an ex-convict-killer. He could still control the evil temper of his heritage; that lesson he'd learned well, the bitter, harsh way he'd learned everything. Yet the fabric of his manhood was raveling steadily away with every new rebuff, and in the gray despair that gripped him he hardly cared to fight any longer. . . .

Boone scrubbed a hand over his whiskered jaw, feeling the trembling in his body and the drawn emptiness of his belly. The street before his eyes swam and blurred; he fought to steady down his numb panic. No food for two days; you're lightheaded is all. He groped for the half dollar in his pocket, closed his fingers over its' hard smooth outline . . . a single coin hoarded from some need for tangible security. It would buy a good supper, let him figure his next move on a clear head.

He stumbled off the curb and walked across to the cafe, holding himself carefully erect. A billow of steamy cooking odors burst softly against his nostrils as he went through the door. He wasn't as yet starving, but Boone MacLaughlin knew a starving man's thoughts as he seated himself at the counter and gave the waitress his order. He fisted his hands together in his lap and stared at them, forcing himself not to think of food . . . panic had humbled his pride. He'd ask Sheriff McKeogh or Sam Ashby for a loan — or old Otto Stodmeier for a swamping job — anything. Those three, at least, would not turn him down. Give up the rest of it, a man had to live; think of that first.

When the waitress set his food before him, he attacked the thick steak with wild appetite. The first edge off his hunger, a belly cramp warned him to take it slowly — and he glanced up to see the waitress regarding his ravenous wolfing with wide-eyed amazement.

Boone stared at her, a forkful of steak pausing short of his open mouth. He hadn't really seen her till now . . . a small, slight girl with very large blue eyes and very black hair tied in a loose Psyche knot, the vividness of eyes and hair contrasting to the ivory paleness of her face. It was a thin little face of a fine-boned structure and it contained an inerasable stain of sadness and hurt that Boone, not ordinarily a perceptive young man, noted at once. She must be around twenty-one, yet whatever bitter travail she'd been passed through had not lessened some quality of urchin-like innocence.

Quick pink mantled her face and she spun quickly away, rummaging aimlessly among some glasses on the back counter to cover her confusion.

Quite suddenly Boone forgot about a job, about food, about his own crucial plight. He tried not to stare at the girl as he mechanically finished his meal, eating very slowly to draw it out. He felt a little giddy and not from hunger . . . didn't know quite what ailed him. And then he wanted to talk and found with an aching desperation that he hadn't a notion of what to say. When had he talked to a girl?

Boone half-formed some words in his mind, forced them to his thick tongue. "I ain't seen you around, Miss."

She gave him a quick wary glance. "I . . .

I guess not." Her voice was a musical murmur.

He cleared his throat a couple of agonizing times and blurted: "What's your name?"

"Christine . . . Powers."

Abruptly the door to the kitchen opened, and Ma Jagger herself came out. A lean, rawboned woman in a staid black gown and with iron-gray hair done in a tight, severe bun, she was the widow of one of the basin's earliest settlers, and herself tough as nails . . . maverick to the core and proud of it. She halted with a big-knuckled hand on her hip, the other removing a thin black cigar from her lips, saying flatly, "Let her alone. You're payin' for a meal — if you can pay for it — not talk."

Boone began sullenly, "I can pay —"

"Then finish it, sonny," Ma said icily, "and when you're done, don't wait around."

Christine Powers was not forward enough even in her own mind to blame the man who had hurt her. Born the daughter of a not-wealthy but highly respectable storekeeper in a small Illinois farming community, she had been painfully shy and sensitive for as long as she could remember. Where other girls had their beaus, their dances, church socials and gossip bees,

Christine had withdrawn farther and farther into a private world of books and dreams.

Then John Bisbee, a young traveling man, had come to town to transact business with her father who invited him to dinner one night. Young Bisbee was different, she'd soon realized. He'd talked, quietly and gently, drawing her out; she found that he had read the books she had, that he was respectfully attentive to her hesitant replies. As time went on, Christine's first caution was overwhelmed by his unslackening consideration and understanding. John Bisbee had lingered in town after his business was finished, and she'd responded to the unmistakable sincerity of his devotion with almost pathetic eagerness. Mr. Powers gave the young man's formal proposal of marriage his hearty blessing.

They had been married by the family minister in a quiet ceremony with only her parents present, and that night took the train West where John's company had assigned him. It hadn't been till the following night, in a shabby little room, that Christine had her first rude awakening. She'd waited hours for her husband, her pillow damp with tears, till he stumbled in soddenly drunk and passed out on the floor.

The following year had been for Christine

a nightmare succession of strange hotels in strange places, of lonely nights, of trying to placate John Bisbee's spiteful, sometimes brutal fits of drunken temper which always ended in his abject, sobbing apologies. Christine had come to painful understanding that the fundamental attraction between them had been a common inability to face life, that what each had needed was a stronger mate who could fill the lack in his partner — and each had only succeeded in becoming mired in the weakness of the other.

It was in a lonely flat on the San Francisco water front that John Bisbee, stumbling up the rickety staircase after a bibulous evening, had toppled over the railing and broken his neck. Christine had gotten work there in Frisco, only to contract pneumonia in the dank, fogbound air. She had lain between life and death for days. A kindly landlady and a charitable doctor had pulled her through and scraped together enough money to start her back East.

But she could not, would not, return to her family. Some flicker of pride had driven Christine Powers to this remote basin where she could bury the past and start afresh under her maiden name. Ma Jagger made a specialty of befriending all kinds of misfits and she'd sized Christine up in one glance and given her a job.

Misfits, Christine thought as she scrubbed down the counter at closing time. Mrs. Jagger and Celsa and me. Father would have a stroke if he could see me now . . . but he'll never know, and that's best. She smiled a little, for in this situation so foreign to her unbringing and temperament, she'd come of late to know something very near to real happiness. Ma Jagger and Celsa Gutierrez, each in her own way, had lent Christine some of their tough, unshrinking strength and warm understanding.

Yesterday when Christine had reported for work as Celsa was going off duty, Ma Jagger had said eyeing both with judicious shrewdness, "I been thinkin' that it's a bad thing for a girl to be livin' alone with that maddog woman killer still on the loose. And Chris, that hotel's no place for a young lady to take board."

Celsa, shrugging into her jacket, had turned her dark, unreadable glance briefly on Christine — had seemed about to speak, but did not.

"Celsa," Ma had said then, bluntly, "why don't you go over to the hotel and pick up Chris' stuff — take it to your place? Two can live cheaper than one, and —"

"That would be wonderful!" Christine had said with impulsive warmth, and then she'd flushed under Celsa's appraising glance. Suddenly she had understood the Mexican girl's deliberate hesitation, and meeting Celsa's eyes, had tried to say without words that the difference was nothing.

Celsa's slow, rare smile had relieved her somber face; she'd said simply, "I would like that."

And it was done. The two of them had talked for hours that night, over coffee in Celsa's little kitchen, and Christine, spending that night on a thin, makeshift straw pallet, had known her first sound sleep in months. They had discussed plans on which she now let her mind happily dwell — Ma would lend them money to enlarge the shanty —

The bell above the restaurant door rang and Christine glanced up, startled, as Sheriff McKeogh entered. She relaxed with a smile, for she liked this elderly man of shrewdly benign eye and wry, penetrating speech.

"Evening, young lady. Didn't mean to startle you."

"Just wool-gathering, Mr. McKeogh. . . . We were about to close up, but if you want a cup of coffee — anything —"

"No, I just —"

"Howdy, Whit," Ma Jagger interrupted, stepping from the kitchen. She paused to scratch a match alight on the woodwork, touch it to her cold cigar.

"Evening, you old curmudgeon," McKeogh answered grinning, for they were old friends. He made a wry face. "Ma, when you going to give up poisoning yourself with those Mex cigars? Fifty per cent rattleweed and the rest —"

"Young lady present," Ma cut in placidly, and McKeogh laughed. Ma blew smoke upward, squinting at him. "You ain't hauling your creaking freight around this late on pleasure calls, Whit."

"No." McKeogh glanced at Christine. "Understand you're living with Celsa Gutierrez now, Miss Powers. A good arrangement — but her place is clear across the tracks. A long lonely walk for you every night. And after what happened to Susan Wells —"

"You planning to escort her home each night, Whit?" Ma asked, screwing up her face mockingly. "Lord Harry, that'll set the local hens a-cackle. Not that you ain't one evil old man."

"True," McKeogh said gravely. "Still waiting for you to marry me and regenerate the devil clean out." He turned to Christine. "I just wanted to give you a word of warning. Stay to the middle of the street, away from the buildings and alleys, when you walk home. You'll be safe enough — just keep your eyes open."

Christine nodded, still smiling at their banter. "Thank you, Mr. McKeogh."

"Whit," Ma said slowly, "what's the chances of you digging up the real killer before those boys come to trial?"

McKeogh eased a hip onto a counter with a sigh, shaking his head. "It doesn't look good, Ma." He eyed her quizzically. "Reckon you're the only one besides me and Celsa and Sam and maybe Otto Stodmeier who thinks Paco and Vicente are innocent. . . ."

Ma Jagger snorted expressively. Those two boys ain't woman-killers, or I don't read men good — which I do. . . . Been two days since Ashby and Celsa brought 'em back. Any idea about that fella who ambushed them out at Deaf Murchison's? Figure maybe there's some tie-in there with the killin'?"

McKeogh stroked his chin. "Ma, the local gossipmongers know as much as I do — which is danged little. It's one of those things you got to sit on a while, hope something will break."

Ma glanced at Christine. "Honey, you ain't interested in the palaver of a couple old mossyhorns. You shake a leg home . . . I'll close up shop."

Christine gave them each a good-night and left the cafe. On weekday nights, the Elkhorn saloons locked up early; the last of the late drinkers had long since straggled into Ma's for coffee and headed home. Now at nearly midnight, the broad length of Jackson Street lay softly moon-drenched, with deep shadows gathering along the boardwalks and building façades.

In a bemused revery, Christine completely forgot Sheriff McKeogh's advice as she turned slowly down toward lower Jackson, heels tapping measured little echoes along the plankwalk. The night was warm, and she took the shawl from her shoulders and switched it back and forth in one hand, humming softly as a breeze gently fingered her face and hair.

Tired but happy thoughts swarmed through her mind, and somehow the memory of the ragged awkward young man who had come in early that evening intruded naturally into them. She'd never before . . . a cowman, certainly, from his rope-calloused hands — but not one of the roistering basin ranchhands. He was different somehow . . . those pale-hard and bitter eyes . . . and yet he hadn't looked at her as some male customers did. She was even sorry that Ma Jagger's protective presence had intruded. He was half-starved and there was something terrible in him just then . . . but it wasn't directed at me, of that I'm sure, she thought.

She felt a small self-irritation. Why did she always judge people in terms of her own shrinking from human contacts? I've got to fight against that . . . look at Celsa; she's not afraid of anything. I'll talk to her, and maybe —

The thought was rudely shattered as she passed abreast of a black alley mouth. Christine caught only a faint shape of movement from the tail of her eye; before her mind could form a cry for help, a hard palm clamped over her mouth and an arm circled her waist, swinging her from her feet.

She felt herself being carried bodily into the alley darkness — heard the shuffling of her assailant's feet and his hoarse breathing. These sensations struck through her paralysis. Fear gathered in her chest and surged from her throat in a scream that was choked ruthlessly off by the smothering hand.

CHAPTER ELEVEN

Boone MacLaughlin, leaning against the livery-stable wall by its broad archway, flexed a long leg to relieve its cramped stiffness, stifled a yawn, hooked his thumbs in his trousers pockets and settled back to continue his long vigil. Watching the big frosted front window of Ma Jagger's Cafe, its square frame of light a final beacon along the dark-blocked buildings.

Boone was beginning to feel foolish and a trifle annoyed with himself. Maybe he was still lightheaded. Otherwise why idle away hours waiting for Christine Powers to leave off work so he could talk to her out of sight of that hatchet-faced old woman? He didn't know, except that he wanted to see her again, hear her musical little voice. He set to rationalizing it: that broken-down one-loop spread of his was a hell of a lonely place for a young man with vinegar — Christine Powers was a pretty little thing, young, and he was sure, unmarried, in a country where the female contingent was still outnumbered. She looked sad and lonely, for sure; give her a sympathetic ear, and — it was worth a try. He felt his pulse quicken, remembering the quick grace of her thin, yet trimly small, body . . . the honing of his appetites was a welcome relief from his troubles.

Sheriff McKeogh came down the street and entered the cafe. Boone yawned again, swearing mildly under his breath. McKeogh would likely palaver a spell, as was his habit, and she'd never get to leave.

But only a minute later Christine stepped out the door, shawl drawn around her shoulders, a slim brief silhouette against lamp-light before she turned into the heavy shadows and headed down lower Jackson. Boone pushed away from the wall and started after her, quartering across the deep dust of the street. He was still twenty yards away when a sudden panic slowed his steps; sweat broke along his temples and palms. Again he felt very young and awkward . . . what in hell did you say to a girl? Anyway, he'd likely scare the shy little thing out of her wits, stopping her at this hour. . . .

Boone tried to steel his faltering intention . . . then abruptly strained his eyes against the banked shadows. The tap-tap of her small brisk steps on the plankwalk had suddenly ceased.

. . . . He heard her scream, muffled and choked, but a scream all the same, brimming with terror. Boone broke into a run. Without slowing pace he lunged across the walk and into the black alleyway, blundering solidly into an unseen trash can. Tripped up, Boone's momentum carried him on and over the obstacle, his arms stabbing blindly out against the darkness; his chin plowed into the ground with a slamming impact.

Scrambling to his feet he heard a soft curse, the sound of running feet. A clatter of boots as a man clambered up and over the high board fence that blocked the alley end. Boone had a dazed glimpse of a sky-lined form topping the fence with a catlike litheness, and then it was over and gone.

"Miss?" Boone said tentatively. "Miss — you all right?"

She made a little throaty sound in the darkness, and he reached out to touch her arm. Felt her shrink away, and then relax with a quiver. He guided her gently out to the moonlight, sent a swift glance up and down the street. The brief commotion had aroused nobody. The girl was standing very close, and, awkwardly he started to take his hand from her arm, changed his mind when her trembling body pressed more firmly against it.

Her face tilted up, a moon-paled oval, and she gave a little gasp. "Oh — it's you."

"Yes'm." Boone added as a hasty afterthought, "Boone MacLaughlin, m'am."

Her breath sighed out audibly. "In another minute — oh, thank goodness!"

"He hurt you any?" Boone demanded fiercely.

"He didn't, thanks to you — Mr. MacLaughlin." She shifted a step away, and Boone dropped his hand. "The sheriff —"

"M'am, thing to do now is get you home first." Boone felt suddenly protective and masterful. "I'll see you to your door — then come back and tell the sheriff. Over in the restaurant, ain't he?"

"Yes." She paused a hesitant moment. "But won't he want to hear from me who that — that —"

"You mean . . . you saw his face?"

"No . . . no. But he said something to me. It — it was like the babbling of a crazy man — but I knew his voice. It was that rich rancher's son, Bannerman —"

"Chet Bannerman?"

Boone's jaw dropped in amazement — and now he remembered tag-ends of gossip he'd overheard earlier. Boone hadn't been to Elkhorn in weeks, and so only today had learned of the rape-murder of Susan Wells three nights ago. Two Mexicans, Vicente Gutierrez and Paco Morales, were being held on suspicion, and Sheriff McKeogh apparently had doubts of their guilt, even if nobody else did. Full of his brooding worries, Boone had listened without interest. But not that talk seemed pregnant with significance. A thing so rare as to provide gossip-fodder for many months, afterward, almost happening again in the same way and less than a week later to Christine Powers, was stretching coincidence way too far. With those two Mexicans safely behind bars, this almost cinched their innocence . . . but Chet Bannerman!

Boone said now with an echo of disbelief, "Listen, you sure?"

"Yes," Christine said firmly. "That Bannerman boy and the other Spanish Spade men often eat at the cafe when they're in town." She paused. "Whenever he is excited, I've noticed — his voice becomes pitched to a kind of nasal whine. Very odd . . . so much so that I couldn't be mistaken!"

It could be at that. Chet Bannerman was . . . strange. No other word for it. Boone recalled that day when they'd thrown the greaser off his jackleg homestead . . . how Chet, almost slobbering with feverish delight, had been set to whip Gutierrez to bloody ribbons with his belt. Attacking a lone girl in a dark alley sure to hell tallied with the same brand of spooky acting to Boone's notion. Maybe being coddled with idleness and too much money could turn a weak son like Chet crazy as a loon. . . .

Abruptly he lowered his gaze to the girl, aware of her meekly trusting him to make her next decision. Again he felt that surge of masculine assertiveness. "Reckon the sheriff had better hear you out now, then."

Together they walked back toward the restaurant. They met McKeogh just leaving, and Christine, a little breathlessly, told the lawman what had happened. McKeogh's face was grim and sharp-shadowed by the moonlight; he listened intently, breaking in with several questions.

"This puts an almighty different light on things," he said finally. "Though if I know General Bannerman, it means that my troubles are just beginning. . . ."

"Sure," Boone said, spitting out his words like a bad taste. "I can see how it'll go. Papa's money and say-so savin' that precious snake's hide. Rich man can buy himself out of hell. All your snivelin' about law and justice, that don't cover the quality. A poor man learns that the hard way. . . ."

His voice dwindled under McKeogh's diamond-hard stare. "You listen, boy. Tomorrow, first light, Sam Ashby will ride out to Spanish Spade. Chet Bannerman will be arrested on suspicion of assault and murder. He will be brought to Elkhorn and put in jail. That rich man's son will stand trial side by side with two penniless Mexicans. If he — or they — are found guilty, he or they will be sentenced according to law."

Boone's lip curled. "Mister, I had a bellyful of your law, remember? — and I ain't forgot how it went." With Christine looking on, he couldn't resist adding with deliberate bravado: "I'm minded to ride out to Spanish Spade myself. Right now. And not to arrest no snake, either!"

McKeogh was silent for a weighted moment, then very softly: "That's Sunday talk, son. I know that, and I can excuse it because I know what a bad deal you got. From hearsay, for I didn't arrive in Elkhorn till after you got sent away. We'll keep what you just said between the three of us."

Boone's face felt burning hot, and he was glad of the darkness. His sullen silence evidently satisfied McKeogh, who now turned to Christine and said gently, "Thank

174

you, Miss. I don't want to rag you with more talk now, shaken up like you are. Come over to the office tomorrow, eh?"

"Yes, sir."

"Lock your door tonight . . . just in case. And don't worry . . . Celsa's got a gun and she's mighty formidable without one." The sheriff smiled at her, shifted a grave look to Boone. "Reckon you don't need any urging to see the young lady home, MacLaughlin?"

Boone muttered something, and he and Christine set off down the street toward its south end. Her hand closed timidly around his arm as they walked, and his lingering sense of surly humiliation evaporated. It had turned out, after all, better than he'd dreamed. His timely intervention had obligated the girl, and she didn't seem averse. He felt a pulse-quickening exultance, his bashful reserve completely forgotten. If he played his hand right, this could lead to something damned interesting.

She was still nerve-shaken, darting quick little glances into the heavy shadows as they passed, and unconsciously she drew closer to him, almost hugging his side. A small breast brushed his arm, a tender calico-sheathed rondure whose touch set up a throbbing clamor in his blood. Then he felt her eyes, so very large and so damned trusting, lift to his face. A wave of sudden shame swept Boone MacLaughlin. He set his jaw then and looked straight ahead, bitter anger compounded of a thousand harsh memories battering back his sense of nagging guilt. Why should you care? Did anyone ever give a damn for your feelings while they done you dirt? No; it's take what you can while you can get it. That's life, and you didn't make the rules. You got a right to pleasure yourself for a change, and by God, you're going to. He shook his thoughts away.

He glanced again at the girl and fashioned a stiff smile, and she smiled back. When he moved his free hand to cover hers where it rested on his arm she did not object. By tacit consent they slowed pace, and so it was a full fifteen minutes before they walked slowly across the tracks and down the long embankment to Celsa's shanty. By the door they halted, and Christine turned slightly so she was facing him, her hand still resting on his arm.

Now go easy, Boone cautioned himself; you're off to a good start. Don't mess it up. He cleared his throat formally. "Reckon I can see you again?"

"I —" Christine's reply was broken short by the door opening. Celsa Gutierrez stood there, fully dressed. Her sharp eyes assessed them both in a flash, lingering with a long cold appraisal of Boone. He had the flushed, guilty thought that this Mex girl read him perfectly . . . or was she only remembering his part in dispossessing her brother of his homestead claim?

Celsa's gaze moved expressionlessly to Christine. "It is late for a girl alone on the street, Chris. I am worried. I was coming to get you. It seems there is no need, eh?"

"Oh — well, I —" Christine paused in her confusion. "I was starting home, you see, Celsa, and something happened —"

"I see," Celsa Gutierrez said tonelessly. "Come in now and tell me about it. After you say good night to Mister Boone Mac-Laughlin."

Christine colored deeply. "Oh — yes. Good — good night, Mr. MacLaughlin."

Boone mumbled good night, turned and tramped up the embankment, his feet digging hard with the raging frustration he felt.

CHAPTER TWELVE

Sam Ashby had lately bought the sorrel he'd been hiring regularly from the livery stable, paying old Burkhauser from an advance on his salary which Sheriff McKeogh had wheedled from the county board. The price was outright robbery, but Sam badly wanted Big Red reserved for his own use; the animal had caught his eye from the first. And it had a leg-reach and staying power that were prime for this work, which had convinced McKeogh.

Sam got the sorrel from the stable and paced him down the street, reining up by the courthouse. McKeogh had just finished breakfast and was standing on the walk, picking his teeth.

"Look at him," McKeogh commented around his toothpick. "Pampered as a lady's lap dog. I suppose you got him snuffling in your pockets for sugar like a hog going after truffles." But there was a trace of envy in the eye as he ran over the horse's rippling musculature. "Ever let him out in a real run? — bet he's a streak of fire. . . ."

Sam nodded with ill-concealed pride as the horse cavorted in a prancing sidestep. "Look at him," the sheriff snorted and then sighed. "All the same, he makes me wish my riding days weren't over. . . ."

Briskly then, he gave Sam his orders. Sam was to tell General Bannerman everything, but not to get tough unless the General did. McKeogh judged that the General, though he'd be furious enough, would offer only token objection to the arrest of his whelp. Surrendering Chet to the law would demonstrate that he had nothing to fear, being absolutely certain of Chet's innocence.

And then Sam, his gaze ranging to the end of Jackson Street, gave McKeogh a wry glance. "Looks like he's not waiting for us to come to him."

McKeogh's eyes sharpened and narrowed on the tight cavalcade of horsebackers who had swung onto lower Jackson. The Spanish Spade crew was turned out in full force . . . fifteen men flanking a spring wagon. General Bannerman sat bolt upright on the wagon seat, unhurriedly pacing a superb team of matched bays down the street. Spectators gathered along the walks, exchanging curious comments.

Sam voiced a speculation, and McKeogh shook his head grimly. "I don't know . . . but I don't like the looks of this. I'll do the talking, Sam."

Coming abreast of the sheriff, Lucius Bannerman brought his team to a halt and his crew tacitly cleared off an open space between the wagon and the sidewalk. Bannerman climbed stiffly to the ground. McKeogh removed the toothpick from his lips with a civil nod. "Morning, Luke. Haven't seen you in a coon's age."

Only McKeogh of all the basin addressed the aloof and austere General so familiarly, and Bannerman's usual betrayal of ruffled poise was a stiffening of his icily courteous manner. Now he ignored the comment wholly, facing McKeogh. He was a spare, slight man who looked crisp and dapper in an immaculate pepper-and-salt suit and a pearl-gray Stetson. He moved with a slight limp and wore a black eye-patch — these and his poker-spine showed legacies of a long military career in the field.

It was strong reminder to Sam that this man stood at opposite poles from his son . . . the one a weak reed easily broken, the other an iron rod which could slightly bend but never shatter.

"Step over here, McKeogh," Bannerman said with a trace of strong and shaken emotion. Sam warily straightened in his saddle as McKeogh came down off the walk to face the General. Bannerman limped to the wagon bed, reached in and took up a corner of tarp ground-sheet covering something bulky. With a flick of his wrist he threw it back.

Sam edged his sorrel a little closer. McKeogh drew a long breath and slowly let it out.

Chet Bannerman lay stretched in the wagon bed, his hands crossed on his chest. His long blond hair was smoothed back from his brow, eyes shut in a pale face erased of its wild and untempered passions. The face, almost, of a very young boy composed for sleep. But a neat small bullet hole high in his chest told another story.

McKeogh slowly removed his hat, a weary and regretful and baffled gesture. "I'm sorry, Luke."

As though he didn't hear the words, Lucius Bannerman began talking in a matter-of-fact monotone. The two shots had roused the entire headquarters shortly after midnight. They had found Chet lying in the middle of the ranch road some fifty yards from the main house. Shot through the heart at close range by a heavy-caliber pistol: so Bannerman summed it up in a few terse syllables. Chet's gun was drawn and one shell expended. The road, its hard surface scuffed by ranch traffic, had yielded no clue. Bannerman had personally questioned each man of the crew, was satisfied that all had been aroused from their bunks by the shots. His son's killer had escaped without a trace.

As he distilled the meat of the General's speech in his mind, Sam let his gaze rove the still, expressionless faces of the crew, studying each in turn. Lastly he met the bland and hooded stare of Milo Squires. The foreman sat his horse easily, hands crossed on his pommel. His eyes met Sam's with a sober blankness.

Bannerman, after a meager pause, said coldly, "Do you have any questions, McKeogh?"

"No, Luke, you wouldn't miss a trick."

Bannerman's single eye was opaque and hard, but his voice trembled: "One week, then. I'll give you one week to the day. If, during that time, you find the man who murdered my son, you will notify me at once."

To this fine arrogance McKeogh only said softy: "And when the week is up?"

"I am not a man without enemies. There are those who would not hesitate to strike at me in any way, including through the one thing I cared for — my son. I have a list of those people . . . can see every name in my mind's eye as clearly as I see you now. If you have not done your duty by this hour next week, I will deal with each of those people in my own way . . . and before I am finished, I'll have a name. And a murderer."

"Luke," the sheriff said gently. "You know how that will go. I'll stop you. Dead, if I have to."

"I will expect you to try."

"No," McKeogh said without anger but very positively. "I'll stop you."

A gust of wind eddied dust around the legs of the grouped horses; one animal shuffled restlessly. Bannerman's bitter eye did not falter. "One week, McKeogh." He drew the tarp above his son's face, turned and swung up onto the wagon seat. Took up the reins and hoorawed the team into violent motion, turning the wagon about in a tight circle across mid-street. The crew fell in behind as he headed at a strong clip back the way they'd come.

"Sometimes," McKeogh murmured, "it all seems to pile up on a man at once. Your wife — Paddy — Susan Wells — now Chet

Bannerman. Four killings in as many months. And what have I found? Not a damned thing — except that Chet might have killed Susie, and I can't take any credit for learning that. I don't have to add that we'll never get the truth from Chet himself."

The harsh self-condemnation of his words shocked Sam; he realized for the first time that McKeogh was plagued by a mounting conviction of baffled failure. "It goes that way sometimes. You've said so yourself. . . ."

"Sometimes," McKeogh answered bleakly, bitterly. "But not like this. It could have been a dozen killings, not just four — it adds up the same thing. Somehow, I'm missing details that no lawman worthy of the name can afford to miss. And that means that an old man with busted guts just can't handle —"

"Quit it, Whit." Sam paused an embarrassed moment. "Something will break."

McKeogh's mood seemed to pass; he nodded briskly, clamping his hat across his thin saddle of white hair. "You'd better ride out to Boone MacLaughlin's. Bring him back here."

Sam was surprised. "MacLaughlin?"

"Yeah. I didn't mention it before . . . After that business last night, MacLaughlin made a halfway threat to go after Chet and settle

184

for the girl on his own."

"Then you think —"

McKeogh made an impatient gesture. "Sam, I just don't know. I figured he was talking to build himself tall with Christine Powers. Playing young Lochinvar to the hilt. I dressed him down in plain language, and I thought it took. Maybe not. He escorted the girl home . . . and then who knows what?"

"Look, Whit. MacLaughlin's bitter, not mean. Not a murderer. He's not the type."

"What type of man is a murderer?" McKeogh countered with a tired smile, and when Sam did not answer: "I hope you're right, Sam. MacLaughlin's got a raw deal all the way along. Your fancy swings to the underdog. Mine too, maybe. But we're not judge or jury. What MacLaughlin threatened, or bragged, before two witnesses, is enough to place him under suspicion. For now, he's also first suspect, until we have more facts. He might not be a killer in the sense you mean and still is guilty."

"How do you mean?"

"MacLaughlin's reaching the end of his string with that rundown spread of his, and the town had declared a boycott — refusing him a loan, a cent of credit. Every man's got his breaking point. Maybe all of Mac-

Laughlin's bottled-up sense of injustice exploded at once — on Chet Bannerman, as things worked out. The kid's dead, but let's not mince words: he was a snotty, arrogant little bastard, made a man itch to hurt him. Often thought that if he ever got the wrong man mad at the wrong time. . . ."

Sam thought that over, saying then: "You didn't tell the General about what Chet almost did . . . to the Powers girl."

"Lord, no," McKeogh said quietly. "You don't tell a man that about his son a few hours after the kid's been murdered."

Sam grunted; that was also good sense, particularly when the incident pointed a cold finger straight at Chet as a possible rapist and killer. The General had worshipped the boy; Chet was all he had after his wife died. The General had spoiled him rotten, pampered his whims, blinded himself completely to what he was making of the boy. When it came out that Christine Powers had identified Chet as the man who'd attacked her last night, how would the General react?

Sam voiced the question aloud.

Very slowly McKeogh shook his head. "Sam — that's a thing I don't even like to think about. When Bannerman learns about that, he'll have to learn about Mac-

Laughlin's part, too. No secret that there was bad blood between Chet and Boone."

"So we get Boone behind bars partly for his own safety?"

"For sure," McKeogh nodded dryly, and slapped Sam on the knee. "Get going now, boy."

Two hours later Sam halted the sorrel on the brow of a long rise which undulated down to a barren flat. When old Bart Mac-Laughlin had first bought this land to develop his sheep ranch, that flat had been watered by a tributary of Tie Creek which divided into several streams and kept it green and lush. Then Spanish Spade, retaliating against the man who would bring in hated woolies, had damned off the tributary where it left the main creek-stem on Spanish Spade land . . . and the flat became a dusty, weed-choked barren.

When Boone had returned from prison, he'd made a pathetic effort to patch the fire-gutted, tumble-down buildings with green logs, odds and ends of lumber. It was a misery place, a thing into which a man could pour a lifetime of blood and sweat and leave nothing but his own bones in its dry dust . . . and only a man sick in his soul would attempt the crazy, dogged, hopeless task of making it anything more.

The grim thought drove disturbingly through Sam's mind as he trotted Big Red down the long slope. He came up on the place from behind, dismounted behind the brush corral and skirted it, keeping his eyes and ears open. Boone's whey-bellied mare was in the corral, so her master wasn't far away. Sam heard scuffling noises from the small barn — a sturdy structure built by the elder MacLaughlin and the only one to survive his venture intact — and headed for it.

He stopped just within the wide entrance, where the big double doors stood open. Boone MacLaughlin, his back to Sam, was spearing wisps of hay on a pitchfork, stabbing at them with a kind of cold, blind, doggedness and tossing them in a pile against the wall.

People in general, Sam guessed, were only unthinking, not unfeeling — smugly righteous and not really cruel. But damned little difference that made this boy who stood in his empty barn trying to scrape up a few remnants of forage. . . .

"Boone," he said quietly.

MacLaughlin turned so quickly he stumbled. Caught balance and dropped the pitchfork handle to the floor, leaning on it.

Sweat gleamed on his lean face, and the eyes were wolfish and harried.

"What do you want?" he rasped.

"Chet Bannerman was killed last night. Shot through the heart. Just outside Spanish Spade headquarters." Sam regretted the bluntness of his speech, but his surface nature wasn't that of a gentle man.

"You come here —" Boone swallowed hard, staring at him — "because you think I done it?"

"No telling about that yet. We haven't made a full investigation. All we know is, you made a threat last night. . . ."

Boone's eyes squinted with the backward race of his thoughts. "O — that. Sure." The full meaning of the situation struck him. "But I didn't kill him! My God — that was just talk. . . ."

"Own a Colt .44, don't you? Killer used a big-caliber pistol."

Dazedly Boone ran a shaking hand over his face. "It's over in the house," he muttered. "Wasn't packing it yesterday. . . ."

"There was bad blood between you and Chet Bannerman — saw that the day we threw young Gutierrez off his homestead. . . ." Sam tried to make his tone reasonable, had the dismal sense he was failing completely.

Boone's fists knuckled savagely around the pitchfork. "Well, damn you to hell — why don't you come out and say it!"

"Wait a minute," Sam said quickly. "McKeogh and I —"

Sam broke off as he sensed the temper, wild and vicious, suddenly triggered off in MacLaughlin. Boone's arm swept back and he threw the pitchfork, threw it like a spear. Sam leaped aside and his foot slipped on damp clay; he fell to a knee, ducking his head as the pitchfork passed above it. The tines hammered into a half-ajar door with a hollow boom.

MacLaughlin started to run past him, hit the damp patch and flailed away his footing, went down in a skidding sprawl. Sam floundered on top of him, trying to grab his wrists. MacLaughlin windmilled savage punches at Sam's chest and face, fighting to heave off his pinioning weight. Sam caught a wrist, and then MacLaughlin's free fist exploded on his chin. Sam furiously yanked his gun from its holster and clubbed MacLaughlin across the jaw. He raised it to strike again — slowly relaxed as he realized that MacLaughlin's writhing body had gone limp.

Sam rose to his feet, touched his aching jaw — his rage passed in a flash of unpleasant insight. He'd come within an ace of beating MacLaughlin's skull in . . . only because the boy had reached the breaking point he probably hadn't before. Sam felt suddenly and uncomfortably close to those basin people he'd been condemning out of his own self-righteouness. "Man has learned something about self-control, human rights and doing unto others since he left the trees," McKeogh had once told him. "A beast lives by an inborn code — and man makes his own code, has a choice whether to keep it or break it."

As a lawman, Sam Ashby was responsible for keeping the code, and more than other men he couldn't afford to forget it for an instant. He had first put on this badge as an escape from a corner he'd let life kick him into — but since then it had become much more. It had changed him a lot — and not enough.

MacLaughlin groaned and rolled onto his side, cradling his welted jaw in one palm. Sam bent to help him to his feet.

"Let's go, MacLaughlin. Make it easy on us both, will you?"

CHAPTER THIRTEEN

Within an hour after Sam Ashby had returned to Elkhorn with his prisoner, the word had spread. The air was full of speculation, excited yet hushed, with a note of unease running through it. Celsa Gutierrez, finishing up her shift behind the restaurant counter, caught bits and fragments of it: ". . . . you see Spanish Spade ride in this morning? . . . his kid was dead, and Spit'n'polish had blood in his eye . . . now Ashby brings in Boone MacLaughlin and locks him up — what's it mean? . . . Well, I heard Chet call MacLaughlin a stinking jailbird to his face once . . . that's how it was between 'em; you figure it out. . . ."

Celsa went impassively about her work and apparently paid no heed to the talk. Actually she kept a sharp ear cocked to every word. Last night, with Christine Powers' narration of what had happened on the way home, Celsa hadn't missed the warm glow in Christine's face as she told of Boone MacLaughlin's part. Celsa had not forgotten how that surly gringo had helped rob her brother of his homestead, and she wasted no liking on him. Quite probably MacLaughlin had carried out his rash threat voiced before the sheriff and Christine, had caught up with Chet Bannerman at his father's ranch and killed him. Celsa didn't care a pin what happened to Boone MacLaughlin, but it would matter deeply to Christine, she knew, and her concern stemmed from the protective role she'd now assumed in the girl's life.

When Christine finally entered the cafe, she was breathless and pale, on the verge of tears. "Oh, Celsa . . . all the way here I heard people talking. It can't be true!"

Celsa slipped off her apron and tossed it on the counter, lifted the counter gate and came to put her arms around the smaller girl. "Don't cry, little one. You know how people talk, probably it is not so bad. Let us go over and see Sheriff McKeogh, eh?"

Ma Jagger came out of the kitchen. "What the hell's going on? What's the kid all weepy for?"

"I will tell you later, Mrs. Jagger," Celsa said. "Listen — I think Chris better not work today."

Ma nodded a puzzled assent. "All right, sure. I can hold things down alone."

As they left the cafe, two women standing by the millinery shop broke off a tidbit of excited gossip, following both girls with stony stares. Celsa did not even glance at them, but couldn't stifle the cold resentment that welled in her. Their voices took up the thread of murmurous excitement behind her, and she could guess how it went: "Those two girls living by themselves — disgraceful! And one of them a Mexican, my dear . . . I needn't tell you what her brother is. I'll just give you one guess about the goings-on in that ugly little shack of theirs every night . . . the latch lifted for every drunken cowhand who comes knocking. Disgraceful. Something simply should be done. . . ."

Celsa quickened her pace, her eyes brittle and cold. She had been aware of similar talk since she'd come to live in this town. She could take it and damn them all . . . but Christine could not stand much more hurt. Always, Celsa thought wryly, she found herself in a maternal position, first to Vicente, now to this gringo girl. Perhaps that was her fate, she thought with heavy self-mockery; Celsa, the eternal mother hen. . . .

They reached the courthouse and turned in at the sheriff's office. The door was propped open to admit a trifling breeze. McKeogh was slacked in his swivel chair, feet propped on his desk and his collar open, fanning himself with a folded newspaper. Sam Ashby was leaning against the wall with his arms folded.

McKeogh swung his long legs to the floor and stood up. "Afternoon, ladies." He saw Christine's pale tenseness, looked sharply then at Celsa.

"We heard some talk," she said. "We think maybe you tell us what is so and what is not." She met Sam Ashby's eye and nodded stiffly. " 'Ow are you?"

Sam smiled briefly and said all right, and Celsa Gutierrez looked away in confusion. She did not know what was happening to her lately, and it frightened her a little. Every time she saw this tall sober-faced man. . . .

Only a few days ago she had still been able to consider Sam Ashby with cold animosity . . . until their expedition to Deaf Murchison's to bring back Vicente and Paco. She couldn't say exactly when it began . . . perhaps when the two of them had been caught in a common danger, cramped together behind a shallow rock with an ambusher's bullets poking about them. Perhaps when she'd come running after him in a flaming, angry fear, that he might corner Vicente and kill him without giving him a chance . . . finding to her vast relief that Sam had risked his neck to take her brother alive. Perhaps when she'd seen blood streaming from a deep cut where Vicente had struck him, and her instant concern by which she'd startled herself more than Sam . . . ruining one of her only two petticoats to tie up his wound.

Her resentment hadn't vanished at once; she was furious at him for abandoning her, her purpose in accompanying him. But as her temper cooled, she'd realized that her unreasoning antagonism had given him no reason to trust her . . . moreover that Sam Ashby's headstrong way of plunging ahead on his self-set course was an exact match for her own disposition. In that moment some warm and kindred rapport had been established, and it frightened Celsa because it was new to her whole experience.

Something else had happened that puzzled her; she wanted to ask the sheriff about that . . . but not while Sam was present. Her face composed, she said now to McKeogh, "The talk was about the dead Bannerman . . . and Boone MacLaughlin."

McKeogh quietly filled in the situation, and then Christine murmured, "May I see Boone, Mr. McKeogh?"

"He's not exactly in the mood for visitors, young lady," the sheriff said soberly.

"I would also like to see my brother," Celsa put in firmly.

McKeogh sighed and lifted down his key ring, tossing it to Sam. "Show 'em the way." Ashby unlocked the cellblock door and held it open, then followed them down the corridor. Paco and Vicente were in the cell adjoining MacLaughlin's.

Though it was Celsa's rule to visit her brother twice a day, she felt each time a renewed shock at how these few days had changed both youths. Vicente's face was drawn and haggard, his eyes dark-rimmed from sleeplessness; a nervous tic had begun in one sallow cheek and he jumped at small noises. Celsa had brought her cousin Rosa to see her beloved Paco — only once — and Rosa had fled sobbing, unable to bear the sight. Paco simply sat in a corner, his eyes haunted and vacant. For no reason at all he would break into sudden laughter or weeping. The relative weaknesses of both were becoming prominent. In Paco, who'd uncaringly laughed and sung his way through life and couldn't tolerate even an hour of sustained brooding. In Vicente, who had looked always to Celsa to shield him from every tribulation, now finding her as helpless as himself.

Celsa quietly spoke to them, then briefly met Sam's eyes as both turned a solemn attention to Christine and Boone MacLaughlin.

Christine pressed her face to the bars, her voice almost pleading. ". . . but I don't believe you did it, Boone."

"Go away." MacLaughlin's tone held a wintry bitterness. He sat on his bunk with elbows on knees and his hands clasped loosely together, staring at the floor.

"Please tell me you didn't do it."

"What do you care?"

Her soft voice faltered. "Have you forgotten last night — so soon? I haven't."

MacLaughlin's pale eyes lifted now, cold and ugly. "You're pretty dumb."

"Please, Boone —"

He swung to his feet with a harsh laugh, leering at her. "You really are dumb. Your friend there had me cold soon's she laid eyes on me. But not you. Ain't you figured it out? Why you think I happened to be so handy last night? Hell, I was waitin' for you myself. Oh, I would of stopped you real polite and said, may I escort you home, m'am, but poor old Chet had nothin' on me. Only he was in a hurry — and I wasn't."

Sam cut in flatly. "That's about enough." He glanced at Celsa, and she, with a look of black fury for Boone MacLaughlin, guided the sobbing girl away. "I could tear that gringo's heart out," she muttered.

"No," Christine choked. "You don't understand — he isn't like that. . . ."

"No? Maybe I don' hear so good. You should not have come here. Better you don' come again."

Out in the office Celsa said bluntly to McKeogh: "I like to talk to you."

The sheriff gave her a long and thoughtful look, then nodded. "Sam, suppose you take Miss Powers home."

When they had gone, he settled with a grunt onto the edge of his desk and took out his pipe and tobacco pouch. "This ought to be private enough." He gave her a brief, humorous regard. "You want to smoke, go ahead."

"No," Celsa said stonily.

"Have a chair."

She ignored the invitation, facing him with penetrating eyes. "I want to thank you for what you do."

McKeogh's hand halted with his pipe halfway to the pouch. "I'm mystified," he said dryly. "What did I do?"

"Ashby came over a couple days ago. To my place. He is driving a wagon full of lumber. He ask me where I want a new room put on my place. I show him, and he set to work."

McKeogh was plainly amazed. "Be damned, begging your pardon. That all he told you?"

"I ask him where he get the lumber, he just say he scrape it up. He does not talk much."

"As a rule, he don't." McKeogh's brows were still knit in puzzlement; abruptly then he grinned. "I get it. You're fishing, aren't you? Want to know whether I told him to do it. Well, Celsa — I didn't. His own idea." His grin held with his shrewd study of her. "You could have asked him yourself."

"Yes, I guess so," she said coldly, then was silent.

"A penny," McKeogh said gently.

"What?"

"Your thoughts. How much are they worth?"

"A wooden peso, maybe."

"More than that," the sheriff said gravely. "Celsa — that man thinks kindly of you."

"You talk like fool," she snapped, feeling the blood mount to her face. "He does me a favor because I take him in once when he is drunk."

"Lady, when will you quit trying to stand all alone?"

She gave him an oblique, chilly glance. "Always think out loud, don' you, sheriff?"

"Yeah. Habit of mine." McKeogh drew a semicircle in the air with his pipestem, pointing it at her. "Look, kid. Listen to me for once. You're a kind and generous person. You want to give everyone something . . . but the one thing you never give of is yourself. Don't be so damn' afraid of your human needs; they're natural to any woman, any man."

"There is a thing I know for sure," she snapped. "I know what a man is thinking of when he talk to me like that."

McKeogh grimaced in rueful surprise. "Lord a'mighty, girl . . . do I look that young? I sure as hell don't feel it. I'm too old for such devious male treachery." He added with a faintly wicked grin, "You know, I could begin to wish I wasn't. . . ."

Celsa bit her lip, struggling not to smile.

"There's a change," he said softly. "A good one, Celsa." Abruptly he stood and shoved his pipe in his pocket, and his voice was serious. "You're one of the lonely ones. I know how that is, so does Sam Ashby. The tailor-made consolations that society offers its other members are not for us . . . something in us makes us carve out our own path. It's harder for a woman than a man . . . too many damn' proper do's and don'ts in a woman's world. It's made you retreat into yourself, afraid of rebuff or injury, like a snail withdrawing into its shell. I know how it is, and I don't blame you. Only remember this: you're not as much alone as you thought. Just quit backing away. Step out of that shell and take someone's hand."

Celsa did not even try to answer that. She fled the office, her face burning. She tried to tell herself that the sheriff had shamed and angered her, but the thought was hollow. McKeogh had forced her battle with herself into the open, and a vast sense of relief was beginning to sing through her.

Oh, but you are a fool — she tried to tell herself contemptuously — over Ashby — a gringo. . . .

But she had found gringos who did not see the racial difference that obsessed her: Christine and Ma Jagger and McKeogh and Sam Ashby. If they did not care, why should she? She recognized the objection as her own final excuse to defend her cherished bastion of lonely pride, and suddenly it was empty. "Step out of that shell and take someone's hand," McKeogh had said. . . .

CHAPTER FOURTEEN

When Sam returned, McKeogh was thumbing through a well-worn Blackstone with dog-eared covers. "There's times," he growled, tossing the book on the desk, "When you got to re-assure yourself. . . . You meet Celsa coming back?"

Sam nodded and slacked into the visitor's chair.

"She say anything?"

"We talked some."

McKeogh scowled at his deputy's reticence.

"You sly old dog," Sam said mildly. "Let me handle my life, will you?"

McKeogh chuckled. "Just pitching pennies, son."

"The Powers girl was pretty upset. Mac-Laughlin gave her some rough talk."

"I heard him." McKeogh tugged his lower lip meditatively. "That either makes him a prime bastard, or a better man than I

204

thought — if he was trying to put the girl off so she wouldn't be touched by whatever happens to him now."

"Didn't work, then. She's on his side hell-to-breakfast."

"Sure," McKeogh nodded. "He's still her very *parfait gentil* knight. Takes a hell of a lot to shake a young girl, sensitive like that, out of her romantic notions, no matter what's happened to her before."

They sat for a time then in morose silence. Sam guessed that McKeogh's thoughts were about as his own, for they'd thrashed the whole situation out earlier. It was like feeling in the dark and finding nothing. The attempt on Paco's life — the ambush of Sam and Celsa — the killing of young Bannerman . . . was there a thread of connection somewhere? They'd batted a hundred possibilities back and forth, and all it boiled down to was that they didn't know a damned thing for sure.

Except that sooner or later, getting wind of the local gossip, General Lucius Bannerman would be riding in on a tornado. McKeogh had already sounded out Abe Burkhauser over at the livery stable, which was situated at the north end of town, to keep a sharp eye out for Bannerman's coming. For now, there wasn't much they could do . . . except wait.

There was a brisk sound of feet on the sidewalk, and two men came in. More trouble, Sam knew at once . . . their visitors were R.B. Fletcher and Preacher Paley.

Fletcher wasted no time on amenities. "The county board just held an emergency meeting — without you, McKeogh — and we have reached a decision. Matters being what they are and rapidly coming to a head, we feel that for the good of the community you should tender your resignation as sheriff, effective as of now."

"You get up that idea all by yourself, R.B.?" McKeogh murmured.

The banker wasn't fazed by a hair. "The meeting was called by my suggestion," he replied in his reedy drone. "Your resignation was also my suggestion. The board voted unanimous approval."

McKeogh slacked back in his chair, regarding Fletcher with a benign, almost genial, eye. "Now as it happens, my office is an elected one, damnfool thing called vote of the people — you may have heard of it. And my term runs for another year. You are sort of grazing off your grounds, R.B."

"As chairman of the board, I am simply conveying our joint request . . . which reflects the will of the people whose opinion so concerns you. Surely, McKeogh, you're not insensible to the sentiment hereabouts concerning your failure to solve the killings of Mrs. Ashby or your deputy — not to mention that Wells girl. Certainly you're sensible enough —"

"Why thank you all to hell."

"— to grasp the gravity of the situation. A dozen people overheard General Bannerman's threat to you of this morning. Now talk has it that you've arrested that Mac-Laughlin fellow on suspicion of young Bannerman's murder. Do you deny it?"

A muscle twitched in McKeogh's jaw. "The affairs of this office are none of your damned business."

"That answers my question nicely. Thank you. And when General Bannerman hears of that arrest, he will ride to Elkhorn with his crew. He will demand Boone Mac-Laughlin. You will refuse to give him up. I need not tell you what will happen then. If you won't think of yourself, think of this town. A decent, law-abiding —"

"Noticed that the other night. When it tried to string up a couple of scared boys. Doubt that they'd make that mistake twice, though — without somebody like you to toll 'em along. . . . Trial by lynching for Boone MacLaughlin, eh? Never fails to amaze me how bastards can always give their bastardy such a high-sounding ring."

Preacher Paley frowned his disapproval, and a deep flush crept up from Fletcher's collar. But he pressed doggedly on: "We do not intend to sit idly by and watch violence explode in the streets of Elkhorn — the lives of decent people jeopardized for the life of that jailbird scum."

"Lives jeopardized," McKeogh asked in his dry, thrusting way, "or business? There's just one ranch of size and wealth in Two Troughs Basin, and its name is Spanish Spade. By pure coincidence, it supplies a good half of your bank's business, R.B. By indentical chance, the other county board posts are all filled by merchants who cut a fat share of their profit from Spanish Spade business. Got no doubt you had a dandy time convincing each other of your inherent nobility, but all the same — you boys wouldn't be kissing Bannerman's tail, would you, R.B.?"

The rude, scathing contempt of it broke R.B. Fletcher's staid armour, and Sam saw the hatred open and naked in his pinched face as he stared speechlessly at the sheriff.

"And," McKeogh continued mercilessly, "you wouldn't just be thinking that with me safely retired, you might be able to appoint a successor who'd meekly bow to your plan, heartily seconded by the sky pilot here, to drop further investigation into Susie Wells's rape-killing so you can safely railroad those two boys into a hangman's noose?"

Preacher Paley, in his black broadcloth, was a paunchy, bloodless-looking man who, except for his burning zealot eyes, resembled an undertaker. "An eye for an eye," he said in a sonorous pulpit voice. "The Mexicans are bondsmen to the Pope of Rome, who is in secret league with the Devil . . . themselves possessed by devils. We must exorcise this evil before it spreads, as men did witches of old. In the name of the church, I second Brother Fletcher's request and ask that you not oppose divine justice."

"I see," McKeogh said, and now he slowly rose, planting his hands squarely on the desk. The words left him in a raging near-shout: "Get out, you pair of jackals! Get out of here!"

They went, and fast. McKeogh made a sound of profane disgust with his tongue and teeth. "The verbal garbage is getting thick enough to cut. Let's walk over to Otto's. A drink might take the bad taste away. . . ."

Among the little knots of citizens gathering along the walks, mounting tension showed in their low-pitched talk and shuttling side-glances at the two lawmen. McKeogh greeted several by name, feeling out their tempers . . . Sam thought the bulk of reaction conveyed a handsoff neutrality. He remarked as much to McKeogh.

"Sure," the sheriff said bleakly. "These aren't bad people. Just that large majority of townsmen who won't take sides till it's forced on them. 'I don't want to get involved; I got to live here.' Play it safe, pasture with the herd, look the other way. The range folk now, they're a different breed — their own men. Only they'd figure this is between the law and Spanish Spade, none of their business. . . ."

"We're in real trouble, then —"

"God, yes. We'll be facing out Bannerman and his crew damn' near alone — when they come. No help here. You saw it . . . a fanatical Catholic-hating pulpit-flogger and a hind-tit man to Mammon. Messrs. Paley and Fletcher, the spiritual and social leaders of the town, taking the lead against us. The two men with the highest responsibility to the public weal thinking only of their own selfish ends. They'll swing the people in their own circles behind them, and the uncommitted will drift with the tide. A few hardheads who do their own thinking will stand with us. That about sums it up."

They swung from the glaring street into the dim coolness of Stodmeier's saloon. A couple of customers glanced at them, quickly finished their drinks and walked out.

"Run home and lock the doors, boys," McKeogh murmured, as he and Sam moved against the bar. ". . . how are you, Dutchy?"

Otto Stodmeier removed his big calabash pipe from his mouth and shifted his vast girth squarely over in front of them. "Goot, Whit. I am speaking of my health. Other things look not so goot."

"Oh, they're falling to pieces nicely. Whiskey."

Sam smiled wryly. "Just something cool."

Otto opened a bottle of cherry soda pop for Sam, poured McKeogh's drink, saying, "Ach. We only can wait. Like I tell you before, you count on me, Whit. And Burkhauser at the livery. Ja, and there are others, but they have not the stomach, though if you ask them —"

McKeogh shook his head. "I won't shame any man into this, Otto. Better think it over yourself. It's going to be rough."

"I am decided," Otto Stodmeier said emphatically. He now leaned his elbows on the bar and crossed his fat arms, saying with ponderous gravity, "I am thinking after what you say the other night." He tapped his gray temple. "So."

McKeogh knit his brows. "What did I say?"

"When you are having a drink here, you mention about an ornament which is torn from the dead girl's neck."

"Oh, that." McKeogh tossed off his drink in a swallow, set his glass down. "I asked Susan Wells's father about it . . . caught him in a sober moment. He said it was just a little heart-shaped locket on a chain . . . was given to Susie when she was little. She had a sentimental attachment to it, always wore it around her neck under her dress. Nothing but a child's trinket, really."

"So. So." Otto's jowls shook with a convulsive excitement. "A child's trinket . . . now the pattern comes clear. This locket, it was not valuable?"

"A few cents' worth of gold colored metal? What's ailing you, Otto?"

"You say the bauble has no value, yet it is torn from the girl as with a brute violence. And the man who has this locket, he is your killer. So?"

"Sure. But he'd have thrown it away when he came to his senses, knowing it could hang him. Some crazy whim made him grab it. Damned if I see what you're driving at."

"Listen. In Germany, in Austria, we have professors of medicine with great interest in the morbid pathology of the human mind. So? Now. When I study at Strassburg, I learn of many instances like that of Susie Wells — the murder victim, the stolen bauble. This locket, this little girl's toy, is in the killer's mind a symbol of the purity, the ideal he has assaulted and violated by his act. To tear it thus from her body is to him a further act of contempt for the ideal. More, he keeps the bauble with him, he does not throw it away. For it now is a symbol of his triumph against a hated thing, it is — it is —"

"A fetish?" McKeogh prompted.

"That is the word."

Sam's scowl marked a struggle to follow Otto's explanation. It sounded pretty far-fetched, he thought. . . . Individuals were different from each other; their acts didn't follow any tidy formula. "Take a pretty shrewd killer to figure all that about himself," he observed.

"Nein, Sam, nein," old Otto said impatiently. "This man acted so because he did not understand his action."

"You saying it was something he couldn't control?"

"That is it, ja — a compulsion."

"Then," Sam said, still doubtfully, "there's a good chance he'd hang into the locket for the same reason?"

Otto nodded emphatically. "It all comes clear in my mind, thinking and remembering those lectures of years ago. It is all one pattern. The girl violated and slain, the symbol —"

"How," McKeogh asked, "could this lunatic commit such an act and otherwise seem normal?"

"The man is not crazy, Whit," old Otto said patiently. "He is sick. In the head, ja? At other times he may be as you and I."

"But he could try the same thing again a few days later, even if it were riskier the second time — just because he can't help himself?"

"Ja. Even if he is basically a coward."

The swingdoors parted and Abe Burkhauser tramped in. He was a stringy, hard-eyed man of seventy, surly and tight-fisted, but he had an iron will for justice and the guts of a tiger to back it. He tongued a stream of tobacco juice at a spittoon without looking at it, saying harshly, "They're comin', Whit. Bannerman and his bunch. Was up in my loft, cut their dust about a half-mile out on the north road, hypered to tell you."

"All right, Abe. Let's get over to the jail."

The four men crossed the street at a fast direct walk, and citizens began fading into the buildings. The street was almost cleared off by the time the lawmen and their allies reached the office. None of them were particularly surprised to find Ma Jagger and Celsa Gutierrez waiting inside.

"Where'n hell you been hidin', Whit?" Ma demanded peevishly. "Get out some shells for them guns."

CHAPTER FIFTEEN

McKeogh went to the gun rack and took down the sawed-off shotguns, handing one to Stodmeier and appropriating the other for himself. Then he reached down a long-barreled Greener for Sam, saying, "We don't want to crowd this thing unless they do. You're younger and faster than us, Sam. If one man does most of the pushing — take him out with that. It'll make any other feisty ones think twice."

Burkhauser was carrying his ancient Henry, and Celsa and Ma Jagger each selected a rifle from the rack. None of the men commented, sensing by the determined faces of the women that objection would be useless. McKeogh broke out boxes of shells from a desk drawer, and they loaded their weapons in silence, except for Celsa. She gave Sam a perplexed frown, and he wordlessly took the rifle from her and filled the magazine. Said dryly as he handed it back:

"Ever fire one?"

"You find out pretty quick," she said grimly.

"Now listen," McKeogh said, laying down his words hard and flat. "You stay inside, Celsa, back of us. You too, Ma. I mean it."

"All right, you mean it," Ma snorted. "I can shoot over your heads, easy as not. I shot at a lot finer targets when Bill Jagger and me first come to the territory, Injun targets, and they wasn't sittin' still."

McKeogh surveyed his small force with a kind of wry satisfaction. "Well, I could have done worse. You're all levelheaded enough that I don't have to tell you not to shoot unless it happens there's no choice . . . All right, gentlemen, let's get out there."

The four men ranged themselves on the boardwalk a few feet apart. McKeogh firmly closed the door and took his station directly before it. Nothing daunted, Ma Jagger and Celsa worked open a window and leaned their rifles on the sill. Sam stood on McKeogh's left and Otto on his right; Burkhauser took a spraddle-legged stance at Sam's left elbow. The stillness of a tense waiting brooded over the deserted street like dynamite on a short fuse. Wind riffled up a furl of impalpable dust which briefly eddied and settled invisibly. Old Burkhauser spat at a crack in the plankwalk. Nobody said any-thing.

Bannerman and his riders were bunched, swinging onto Jackson Street at its north end, but they fanned out gradually as they came on. Gun-hung and ready, the lot of them, and Sam noted the pre-arranged way they heeled their mounts around facing the courthouse, sidling out into a double skir-mish line. It was a big outfit, Spanish Spade, and these were hands both old and new, unconsciously partaking of the ruthless pride that only a big and wealthy ranch could afford. A quality compounded of many things: safety in numbers, a bully's arrogance, a fierce loyalty to the great entity of Spanish Spade. Ordinary men, singly and by themselves, but their weaknesses were absorbed and collectively erased by a com-mon purpose. The fact that they'd held Bannerman's insolent pup in no affection was irrelevant here: Chet had been Spanish Spade. What it added to was that these men wouldn't break or run . . . they'd have to face it out.

Lucius Bannerman had reined out ahead of the others, his bay halted short of the plankwalk. "You have the killer of my boy. I want him, McKeogh."

Not a request, an order. McKeogh opened

the negotiations mildly: "Luke, MacLaughlin hasn't been proven guilty by a far piece."

"Ah," Bannerman breathed. "That's what I wanted to hear. My cook came to town for supplies earlier; he brought home a rumor . . . no more. But it set me to thinking on things I'd heard. I know nothing of this McLaughlin except by reputation — and his, I understand, is a bad one. Chet had run afoul of this fellow once or twice. That, added to the fact that you saw fit to arrest him immediately after my visit this morning, indicated a tie-in. And now you've confirmed it."

"Hell, I didn't intend to deny it," McKeogh said irritably. "Particularly since you've made up your mind."

Bannerman's thin hands knuckled savagely around his reins as he leaned forward. His voice was a hiss. "Don't bandy words with me, McKeogh. All I want to know is why MacLaughlin did it — before we take him."

"Sure you want to hear it?" McKeogh asked tonelessly.

"What do you mean?"

"This morning, Luke . . . I didn't tell you then that Sam Ashby was about to ride out to Spanish Spade. To arrest Chet."

"Arrest . . . ?" The rancher's face darkened. "I don't doubt it. Chet was wild, no question of that. He rode in late last night before —" Bannerman's voice broke, took up on a steel thread. "All right. What did he do? Break a window? Touch off a string of Chinese firecrackers? Ride his horse into a saloon?"

"Nothing like that, Luke," McKeogh said bluntly. "He attacked a girl — dragged her into an alley. If Boone MacLaughlin hadn't happened along, there's a good chance that girl would have turned up like Susie Wells."

The blood surged to Bannerman's face, melting away his first shocked disbelief. "You . . . lie."

"The girl heard his voice before he broke away. She'd heard it before, when Chet came to Ma Jagger's — she works there —"

Bannerman's lightning gaze found Celsa's face in the window. "*That* girl?"

"No. The other waitress. Christine Powers."

Bannerman's narrowed eye shuttled a questioning glance over his shoulder. Milo Squires sat his shortcoupled bronc at ease, hands crossed on his pommel. His sleep eyes were unchanged, only a faint tension in his squat frame telling of a leashed alertness. He shrugged one shoulder.

"Christine Powers? — just some trash

drifted into town a month or so back, Genril. Ma Jagger give her a job, and I heard she'd moved in with the spic, there. She come to Elkhorn broke and with nothing much but the clothes on her back. That'll give you an idea. No better'n she should —"

"Boy," Ma Jagger razored across his speech, "I got a tight bead square on your shirt pocket, and my finger's getting God-awful nervous. You just stick to the facts, the cold facts. I don't know Genril Bannerman, and he'd as lief not know me. But allowin' for his present state, he's still a gentleman. I don't make no mistakes about men. And a gentleman don't judge a woman on hearsay slime. So boy, you keep your dirty tongue still or stick to the facts. I won't say it again."

A moment's silence trickled away into long seconds, and Sam settled a narrow watchfulness on the Spanish Spade men. Always his eyes came back to Leo Stapp, that intense, burning wire of a man who'd been Chet Bannerman's only real friend. Chosen allies ready for any vicious frolic that struck their fancy. Leo — undersize, dirty, stupid — with a hair-trigger temper and the reflexes of a cat. And Sam saw the suppressed wildness in his fevered eyes as

221

he sat his horse next to Milo Squires, his flushed fury sawing at a thin leash of restraint.

If a man went out of control first, it would be Leo Stapp. And Sam watched him.

Meanwhile, Squires, apparently unfazed, gaze Ma Jagger a full brunt of his hooded stare. But he held silence now, and Lucius Bannerman turned a puzzled eye on Ma — gave her the faintest of respectful nods before returning a hard attention to McKeogh. Ma's speech had obviously shaken the General's composure; his voice shook with uncertainty.

"I can't believe that of my boy . . . I won't believe it. The girl must have been mistaken — or she made more of the incident than it warranted. Why didn't you tell me before — ?"

"You'd have believed it no more than you do now," the sheriff said steadily. "And I needed a breathing space to get Mac-Laughlin in jail . . . for his own safety."

"But you had a reason for suspecting MacLaughlin . . . else why arrest him?"

"MacLaughlin — last night, after he helped the girl — made what sounded like a threat. Just sounded. I was there, and it was windy talk. Anyway I think so — hope you will too, Luke. I'm not holding back a damned thing."

Bannerman drew an unsettled breath. "No — I don't believe you are. . . ." But he said with a dogged disbelief, "The girl was wrong about Chet. My God, McKeogh — do you realize what you said? That my boy was the same one who did that hideous thing to the Wells girl?" Again the feral rage was mounting uncontrollably in the man. "That's a rotten way to hit a man, McKeogh. Through his son. His dead boy —"

"Luke," McKeogh said with finality, "I'm sorry as I can be. But that's how it stands. I only ask you, don't make a move now you'll regret the rest of your life — if you live. You need time to think . . . cool off. I don't believe that Boone MacLaughlin's a killer, whatever you may have heard. I'll worry out the truth of the matter, but I need time. And when I find the man . . . let the law have him. When you come to Elkhorn again, come alone. Because if you come at me with a pack on your heels — now or later — there'll be a lot of dying right on this spot. And you'll be dead before you reach this door. I swear it, Luke."

McKeogh's cold, passionate sincerity seemed to jar a thrust of sanity against Bannerman's pain and grief and rage. Sam felt the man's agony — could pity him even this minute.

"Luke," McKeogh went on, "here's something to occupy you. Go on home. Look through Chet's stuff. His clothes, his gears. There's a —"

Then Leo Stapp's self-control frayed away as he saw the situation slipping into McKeogh's hands, and he choked a frenzied, "No, by God!" as his gun blurred from holster.

It was over before a man could think — the roar of Stapp's pistol, and the sheriff grabbing at his chest and his shotgun clattering to the walk.

No man could have beaten that nervous speed — the bleak conviction flashed through Sam's mind as he tilted up his ready Greener. The roar of it blasted down the echo of Stapp's shot, and the heavy charge smashed Stapp from his saddle and sent him into the dust.

The nearest riders held in their skittish broncs. Other than that, not a man moved . . . watching Leo Stapp kick away his life in the moiling dust. The buckshot had taken him full in the throat, and his struggle was a brief one. McKeogh had been right. The bloody retaliation held the others as nothing else could have done . . .

for an instant the whole thing had almost broken wide open. Sam fought to hold that fact, the grim necessity of his action, against a tight lift of sickness.

He spoke then, hearing his voice come calm and measured: "There's another load in this thing . . . for you, maybe, Milo?"

This as the foreman shifted his weight, a leather-creaking movement that bought the Greener's twin muzzles to sight on his board chest. Milo Squires merely stared back. But he was careful not to move again.

Only then did Sam look at McKeogh.

The sheriff had slipped down against the building, his knees drawn up and shirtfront covered with blood. Eyes closed and his breath soughing in and out as a harsh rasp. Sam, unable to tell whether he was conscious or not, spoke McKeogh's name — no response.

"Otto — you know doctoring. Look to him."

Celsa now hurried outside, knelt to support the sheriff's head while Stodmeier opened his shirt. Sam's face and body felt clammy as he kept a stiff attention on Spanish Spade. As the taut silence dragged out, he finally said sharply, "Otto!"

"Ja, ja. He is alive, just about. We get him inside. Miss, take his feet, please."

While they bore McKeogh into the office, Lucius Bannerman sat his horse dull-eyed, oblivious to the unwavering threat of Abe Burkhauser's Henry. And now, Sam knew, it was all on his shoulders. McKeogh, his friend and mentor, had left him lonely heir to the whole explosive business. Sam felt the swarming impact of self-doubts that hadn't assailed him since his comeback from the debauching grief of his wife's death. Even McKeogh, with his deft command of words and men, had lost control of the situation at the moment when it had seemed that he'd successfully quelled it. How could he, Sam Ashby, a man of spare insights and fewer words, take it over?

He knew only that he had to try, do the best with what he had. This was a crucial moment for the man he'd sought to become, with McKeogh's help . . . a man who could direct his stubborn energy into something larger than self-interest. If he couldn't see out this thing that his friend had left unfinished, that new Sam Ashby was a straw man, helpless to stand alone.

The Spanish Spade men were still badly shaken by the unexpected flurry of violence that had taken the life of one man, perhaps of two. It was one thing to work to such a point, another thing to see it happening.

Even Lucius Bannerman was mute and waiting. Sitting very straight on his bay horse, his fine features seeming old and shrunken in a gray mask.

Crowd it hard, Sam thought. That's the only way, now. . . . "General, this was a damned-fool thing. If McKeogh dies, it'll be on your head, your soul."

Bannerman's eyes flickered dully. "You're a steady-sounding fellow, Ashby. I wonder — just how much of a rock are you?"

Behind Sam's iron concentration, memory prodded like a small still voice. What had McKeogh started to say before Stapp had cut loose? Luke, here's something to occupy you . . . look through Chet's stuff. . . .

That was it — the locket. Susie Wells' locket in the possession of the man who'd killed her. The symbolic trinket he would not have discarded, if Otto Stodmeier was right. McKeogh had intended to divert the General's attention by suggesting a search of Chet's belongings for the missing ornament. Sam was still skeptical of Otto's theory, but he couldn't afford to pass up any possibility, however slender, that might head off more violence. If nothing else, it would provide a breathing spell . . . give Bannerman a chance to reason coolly.

But if he doesn't find the locket! That

would worsen matters, Sam knew bleakly; certain then that his dead son had been falsely accused of a degraded crime, Bannerman would have added fuel for his vengeful rage. Yet if found, the trinket would be shattering evidence that the General could not deny. It would cruelly cut the ground frum under the man, twist a knife in his raw grief — but there was far more to consider than one man. Take the chance, Ashby — you got no choice, he told himself.

"General," Sam said positively, "you're likely to find out a lot about me without you sit still and hear me out."

And he talked for a full five minutes, halting now and again to dredge his mind for the proper words. It wasn't easy, but he was making it clear enough to every man — he could see that in their intense, frowning concentration. As though they were eager to find an excuse, however flimsy, to back off from this deadly tableau without losing face.

Without expression Bannerman listened, nodded agreement with surprising readiness. "You're right about one thing, Ashby . . . it will be worth knowing whether or not this accusation against my boy is a blackleg lie. If I find that it is — I will be back. And then, my friend, it will be you

who learns something about Lucius Bannerman."

CHAPTER SIXTEEN

After getting McKeogh over to Dr. Enright's office, they were all soon relieved by Enright's cautious verdict that the sheriff would live, though it might be touch-and-go with him for a time.

"I warned him to slow down after that horse threw him last year," the doctor said almost angrily. "Hope he has the sense to retire after this damnfool junket. Damned if I know what drives a man . . . or the rest of you." Enright surveyed the five of them intently, one by one — Sam, Burkhauser, Otto Stodmeier, Ma Jagger and Celsa Gutierrez — and shook his head. "Quite a few of us are not necessarily lacking in principle, only courage." He paused with an air of perplexed sadness. "Did I say 'only'?"

"Never you mind, Doc," Ma Jagger said grimly. "You'll be needed otherwise, patchin' up survivors. . . ."

Because there was no more they could do

here, they all headed back to the sheriff's office. Celsa walked by Sam's side, tall and sturdy and straight, with wellsprings of inner strength Sam was only beginning to appreciate. He wanted to tell her that, and more. Tomorrow maybe if he could find the words . . . would there be a tomorrow?

Meantime they could only wait on Bannerman's return. If his search of Chet's room and clothing and miscellaneous gear turned up nothing, they'd have gained only a few hours' grace till showdown. One thing was certain: that search would be conducted with meticulous care, because when all was said and done Lucius Bannerman was a man who would face the truth unflinchingly, whatever the cost.

Sam had hoped he might take his crew with him, thus giving them an opportunity to spirit MacLaughlin out of town to a safe hiding place. McKeogh, to whom the law was a creed no matter how flexible he'd made it at times, would not have approved of this tactic, which amounted to weakness before men who would flaunt the law. But Sam was feeling his own way now, and all things considered, he'd thought the idea made sense. Only Bannerman might have foreseen it, for he'd left his entire crew behind. Some of them were now loafing on the hotel porch, others had tied up in front of the Blackjack Bar. Leo Stapp's body had been removed to the undertaking parlor . . . only dark dried stains marked the scuffed dust where he had died, victim to his own uncontrollable passions.

Entering the office, Sam laid his rifle on the desk and said to the others, "Might as well relax. We —"

He cocked his head as a weird sound began in the cell block, a low, crooning moan which mounted with a kind of wailing intensity.

"Paco," Celsa observed wryly. "He is one of us with not so much pepper in the belly."

Old Burkhauser gave a grim snort of laughter.

"I'll try to quiet him," Sam said resignedly and took down the keys, unlocked the cellblock door. Celsa followed him down the corridor.

Paco Morales was on his knees, his hands gripping the bars. His eyes were glazed and his body was racked with shuddering moans. A thin line of spittle crept down his chin from his slack mouth. Sam regarded him with no patience; in the past few days he'd listened to Paco's abject, broken terror for hours on end.

Now he began to gibber wildly, "Por Dios,

Meester Sam, do not let Meester Squires get poor Paco, don't let him —"

Sam angrily banged the key ring against the bars, and Paco ducked his head, cringing. "Damn it, get it through your head they're after MacLaughlin, not you! So far, your worthless hide hasn't got a scratch. You want to pray, pray for Whit McKeogh. He's wounded, and bad. You hear that, Gutierrez?" Sam turned his fury and comtempt on the other two. "You hear it, MacLaughlin? A better man than the lot of you, and he's apt to die for it. . . ."

Boone MacLaughlin was crowded against his cell door — his face pale and sweat-shining, which he now turned slowly away. Vicente Gutierrez sat on his bunk and hung his head, his hands clasped between his knees. He did not look up.

"Think about it," Sam said thinly. "All of you. . . ." His voice trailed off to a long blank pause. Then, quietly: "Paco. What did you say before?"

Paco, open-mouthed, shook his head slightly.

"About Squires . . . Milo Squires. Don't let him get me, you said. Why?"

Paco scrambled to his feet and backed away, mutely shaking his head, his liquid eyes filled with pure terror.

Sam fumbled a key into the lock, opened the cell door and grabbed Paco by the scruff of the neck, shaking him furiously. "What did you mean about Squires? Bannerman was heading the outfit, and he's after Mac-Laughlin. But you're afraid of his foreman . . . why? Answer me! Damn you!"

Paco's body was limp and unresisting in his grasp, only the head moving slowly and doggedly back and forth in negation. Cursing, Sam flung him against the wall.

Celsa gasped her shocked protest, and Sam's blazing wrath cut relentlessly across it: "There's something been nagging at the back of my mind. Something I can't give a name . . . something tied up with Paco here . . . and maybe with Milo Squires. I can't put my finger on it — but by God, he's going to talk now or I'll break his damned neck!"

Celsa searched his face a long moment, and then she stepped into the cell and knelt by Paco, talking to him in rapid Spanish, her tone low and earnest. Morales covered his face with his hands and rocked to and fro in his mute misery. Finally he blurted a terrified reply, and now Celsa raised a troubled face.

"He cannot tell a thing, he say. It has to do with an oath he give. He is more afraid of what happens if he break it than he is of you. He will not talk. I ask you, don' hurt him, please. It will do no good, an' it only make you sick whenever you remember it. Look at him now . . . believe what I say."

Sam swung away, knotting his fists at his side, reaching for self-control. Celsa was right. Yet he wanted to smash out at something in his frustration — somehow he curbed the impulse and tried to think coolly.

He fumbled backward in memory to a rainy night when he had barged into Stodmeier's saloon in a hot vengeance to find his wife's killer. He tried to reconstruct that scene. Milo, half-lying on a table in a drunken doze, his head pillowed in his arms . . . or had one of Milo's hands been concealed beneath the table? And Paco — Paco had been sweating profusely on that chill, damp night . . . had he also been rigid with suppressed tension, his voice high-pitched with it? Sam frowned and scrubbed his palm across his forehead. In his state of mind then, he'd had no eye for such details, but some part of his mind must have registered them. His whole recollection of that night was nightmarish and dim and unreal. A few fragmentary impressions were crystal-clear, the rest was muddy and chaotic, and he couldn't be certain of anything. Yet he

235

felt with an overwhelming excitement that he was downwind of something important.

His thoughts leaped ahead to a more recent night, when Milo Squires had led a mob that had come within an ace of lynching the two Mexicans. And he clearly recalled his puzzled assessment of Milo's action. Outwardly bland as butter, Squires possessed a deep and concentrated nature. Sam had known after their fight on that morning of months ago that the man would be capable of long-storing a grudge, hating like an Indian, while coldly biding his time to square accounts. Again, Sam had noted, though only in passing, that the Spanish Spade foreman hadn't been gripped by the mob fever he'd skilfully organized and directed toward a lynching bee. . . .

Why? Because Milo had only seized on a tailor-made opportunity to seal Paco's lips for good, and for a private reason?

Sam realized that Otto Stodmeier was standing at his side, nodding gently. "You are right, Sam. I had noted it from time to time . . . before the trouble which landed him here, Paco sometimes behaved strangely. Often he did not come to work, or showed up drunk. Was this, I wondered, the gay and joyous Paco? When I asked him what is wrong, he would not answer, and so

I left him alone, judging this to be a private matter which is none of my business, ja? So. But maybe I am wrong."

"We all were wrong," Celsa said then, somberly. "Everyone in Mextown knew that Paco had changed. He was never like this, we all said, and so he must be in bad trouble, having as he does the heart of a rabbit. And to protect poor Paco, we say nothing to any gringo, any outsider. That is how it was. . . ."

Sam moved to Paco's side and dropped a hand on his shoulder, and when Paco cringed away, Sam said gently: "I won't hurt you. Come along. We're going to see the sheriff. . . ."

To Celsa's anxious question, he added soberly: "That can't be helped. If anybody can make him talk, it's Whit McKeogh. And he's got to talk. Got a hunch this thing goes deeper than any of us know. . . ."

They were in luck.

McKeogh's cubbyhole of a hotel room was plainly furnished, bearing the Spartan imprint of its tenant's personality. And even now, looking strangely frail and helpless beneath his blanket, the sheriff's driving will had forced him to a thread of consciousness, and he held it tenaciously. Listened to

Sam's story and impatiently glared away Dr. Enright's insistence that he rest.

Only Celsa had come with Sam and his prisoner; she stood by the trembling Paco, resting a firm hand on his arm while Sam crouched down by McKeogh's bedside and quietly explained.

When he had finished, McKeogh wordlessly lifted a hand from the coverlet, beckoned feebly. The Mexican boy came over like one in a trance and knelt down, his face on a level with the wounded lawman's.

"Paco, what of this oath you have taken?" the sheriff whispered. "Tell me a little about that. Does your priest know of it? By what did you swear?"

Celsa and Sam exchanged startled glances at the sheriff's fluent Spanish, and Sam shook his head. Even he, Celsa realized, hadn't seen all the many facets of this enigmatic and accomplished man. Then, following the conversation between McKeogh and Paco, she translated the gist of it to Sam in a low whisper.

". . . Senor Whit, do not ask me that, I beg of you."

"Paco, I have known you since I came to this basin eight years ago. When you were a brown imp of a boy, even then, we were

238

friends. Is it not so?"

Paco's tense body seemed to relax visibly. "Yes."

"Often I gave you advice in the hard growing-up times of a boy's years, but I did not censure you when you ignored my heeding . . . which was always."

Paco weakly returned the sheriff's smile. "Not always, senor."

"That is true. And when you did as I advised, did you ever have regret?"

"No, never. The saint smiled on me." The old gay and cocky Paco was flickering through. "Father Francisco found my confessions less lengthy."

"How long since you have been to confession, Paco?"

Paco Morales flinched a little; his face tightened. "A year. Maybe more. I do not know."

"Your padre is bound to secrecy by the confessional seal, yet you feared to tell even him — of this thing on your soul?"

Paco burst into tears. "It was a terrible oath, Senor Whit! You do not know — !"

"I know more than you think, amigo mio. Your Church offers hope of redemption from every manner of sin, Paco. Penance — and absolution. But a man must seek what is offered. It is not for me to judge the gravity of your sin, if any, but it is certain that you have fallen into grave error. . . ."

McKeogh continued in that vein, quietly and reasonably, not rushing Paco, giving him time to absorb each point. Perceptibly the boy began to relax — and his confidence in the sheriff as a fair-dealing friend did the rest.

Then he began to talk, telling of that stormy night when Milo Squires had burst into Otto Stodmeier's saloon. Told how the Spanish Spade ramrod had feigned a drunken sleep while he held a gun on Paco beneath the table, forcing him to give the lie — to alibi Squires' whereabouts for the previous hour to the first person who came in. Luck had run in Squires' favor, in that the bad weather had held the citizens in their homes; business had been so poor that Otto had left early, leaving Paco to handle any late customers, clean up and lock the place. Nobody had entered during the hour and a half after Otto had gone home — till Squires came. And finally, thanks to the storm, nobody had seen Squires ride in — only Paco knew the real time of his arrival.

Ironically, the first person to enter after Milo, to hear the false alibi from Paco's lips, had been Sam Ashby himself. The terrible part, to Paco, had happened after Sam had left. Squires had put his gun against Paco's head and forced him to swear by the Holy Virgin that he'd never breathe a word of the truth, else forfeit his hope of salvation. Overcome by the very real terror of the moment, Paco had sworn the dreadful oath.

Celsa, knowing her people and with the added insight of an independent mind, understood clearly Paco's long and tortured silence. The old beliefs, the dark and ancient rites that had ruled this land long before the coming of the padres, had never been eradicated, only modified by the newer faith. In Paco's simple mind a thousand superstitions rioted in utter confusion, and their sum was far stronger under subsequent reflection than the dangers of reality. And bound by an oath whose breaking, he was certain, would merit him eternal damnation, Paco had existed in his private hell rather than speak out. These things she explained to Sam as best she could.

Paco had broken down and was weeping quietly. And Sam, realizing the inner torment of which Paco was at last relieved, couldn't find it in himself to blame the boy. Sam's face was grave and still beneath McKeogh's probing glance, and the sheriff faintly nodded his approval.

"Welcome to civilization, Sam," he said

241

gently, and then to Paco: "I'll have Father Francisco brought from Mextown, son. You'll tell him everything, as you should have done in the beginning. He would have explained these matters had you only asked. . . ."

"Gracias," Paco choked. "Gracias, Senor. . . ."

"There's part of it set up for you, Sam," McKeogh whispered weakly. "All I can do. Rest of it's up to you. All I can do. . . ." His eyes closed then.

"Ashby, the man needs rest now," Dr. Enright said firmly.

In the hallway outside McKeogh's room, Celsa halted Sam with a hand on his arm. "That *segundo* Squires," she said soberly, "it was he who kill your wife and the deputy Delaney?"

"Seems that way." Sam wondered at his own cold and positive calm. "That, and he's the one who figured to gun Pace in his cell after failing to get him lynched. The one who pinned you and me down out by Deaf Murchison's. Milo followed us there, worked ahead of us and couldn't resist the chance to lay up an ambush for me — place as lonely and isolated as that was perfect. Was me he was after when he shot Nancy by mistake — he hates my guts that much

242

and more. . . . Nailing me, he would have gone after Pace. Likely he'd have had to kill you and Vicente, too, but he didn't care — he'd already killed twice."

"You are sure of all this?"

"It had to go something like that. Milo was fairly sure of Pace after he got that oath out of him . . . not so sure, I reckon, that he wouldn't have put a bullet in him later on. Except that if Pace had turned up murdered, after giving an alibi for Milo, it would have looked damned odd. Milo thought — then — that that would have cut it too fine — he didn't know how deep he'd finally get sucked in. He decided to coast along, play it cautious for a time. . . ."

"But why then did Squires change his mind?"

Celsa listened intently as Sam told her that Squires had been in town the night Susie Wells was raped and killed. When he'd seen that Pace was one of the two accused, he'd seen the occasion as a prime opportunity to shut Paco's mouth for good — so on the spot, Milo had taken charge of the mob, goaded up the lynch proceedings. McKeogh and Sam had stopped that . . . and then Squires had seen something else. That Paco, headed for a hang rope as a woman-killer, was apt to crack under the strain when he gave the priest his last confession, or even before. The oath Pace had given Milo, strongly as it held Paco's simple mind, would surely not bind him for long under these circumstances . . . and sooner or later Paco would tell what had actually happened the night Sam's wife and Paddy Delaney had been killed. Then Squires had really begun to run scared — knew that he had to make sure Paco would never talk.

Celsa said accusingly to Paco, "You knew that it was the segundo Squires that sought your life, and you held silence even then?"

Paco Morales' eyes were haunted. "I could not tell what I guessed, not without telling all the rest. Por Favor, Celsa, there was a thing I feared more than I feared Senor Squires. At times I thought of telling the truth, but always I was afraid."

"You must make this thing right now," Celso told him severely. "You must make a lawful confession and sign your mark to it."

Sam had followed the meat of this exchange in Spanish, and now he shook his head. "Too late. People might have listened, before what happened to Susie Wells, though it was Milo's word against a Mexican's. Now it'll be Milo's word against an accused rapist-killer who's a Mexican. You know how it'll go, well as me, Celsa — maybe even better."

She nodded bleakly. "I know. So what we do, Sam?'

"You and Paco," Sam said slowly, "are going back to the jail — and stay there. I'm going to talk with Milo Squires. We still don't know who killed Chet Bannerman, but I have to gamble there's a tie-in. Milo's the only killer we're sure of. Too damn' much I can't even guess at, and I'm working against time now. Bannerman'll be back shortly. . . .''

"Squires is a very mal hombre," Celsa said doubtfully. "The truth, can you get it from him?"

"I'll get it," Sam said flatly.

Christine Powers arrived at the jail a few minutes after Celsa returned with Paco. Christine stated her mission firmly, overriding Celsa's baffled and near-angry objection.

"Hasn't the gringo MacLaughlin done you enough hurt?" Celsa demanded. "Go on home, *nina.* Stay away from him. He is no good for you."

All of those in the sheriff's office, Stodmeier, Burkhauser, Celsa and Ma Jagger, were eyeing Christine with an alien puzzlement, but it only seemed to stiffen the determination which had brought Chris there.

"You don't understand him, Celsa," she flung out defiantly. "None of you do. And I will talk to him, so please don't stand in my way."

Celsa regarded her for a long sad moment. "Nobody can stop you, Chris," she said at last, wearily.

The door leading to the cell block was open, and Christine briskly marched into the narrow corridor and down to Boone MacLaughlin's cell. She glanced at the two Mexican boys in the adjoining cubicle, then ignored their apathetic curiosity. They would hear what she had to say, but she didn't care. All that mattered was that Boone listen.

Boone was sitting on his bunk, his shoulders hunched and his elbows on his knees, his hands laced together loosely. His expression was hard and distant and unrelenting.

Christine pressed close to the bars, whispering, "Please don't pretend any more, Boone. We both know how it was between us from the start —"

"You're out of your head, girl," he muttered. "Go away."

"Not this time, my dear. I've run away

too often . . . all my life. I'm only now learning that a woman in need doesn't run. She had to fight for what she wants . . . or beg. Please don't make me beg."

"I said all I had to say." The indefinable strain of a hidden struggle marked his words.

"Oh Boone, don't you see? — I know how you've felt because I felt the same way — the hurt, the suspicion, the fear of being hurt one more sorry time —"

"You don't know anything about me," he stated harshly.

"I know everything. Mr. Ashby told me all about you when he took me home a while ago — but I'd already guessed at a lot of the truth."

Slowly Boone came to his feet and stepped closer. They stood inches apart, but he made no move to touch her. She saw the torment in his face. "You still don't understand. The reason I waited for you last night —" he swallowed hard — "was what I told you a while back. That's the truth, too." A storm of bitterness roiled beneath his low voice. "Now what do you think?"

"Not much . . . except that you had to hide the real reason from yourself because you could no longer trust a decent feeling. The same way you growled at me today to hide something else — that you were afraid for me, not yourself. You were trying to drive me away — as you are now — without letting me know the truth. But Boone, that's wrong! I need to know the truth because I need to share with you — I need it so badly!"

A tight hard smile flicked at the corner of his mouth. "I botched that. Way I botch everything I put a hand to."

He reached blindly and gripped the bars, and she heard a bitter sound break in his chest. Watched him fight it back — but it rose into his chest and choked from his lips, and then the terrible and wracking sobs of a grown man shook him. Christine drew his face to hers, whispering, stroking his head.

Shortly he drew back, his expression gruff and shamed.

"You needed to do that."

He didn't deny it. But he growled, "Ain't cried since my Ma died. I was only four then. You better know that."

"I know all I need to. . . . You're strong, Boone. You had to be, to take all you have taken and stand up to it. I need your strength, Boone. I need you. You see — I'm not strong. That was the trouble. . . ."

She told him of her early life, about her mistake with John Bisbee. Told him without restraint, feeling a strong warm relief flood through her and knowing she'd closed that chapter in her life for good.

"You can forget about all that," Boone said flatly. He took her hand in his, and his eyes were very sober. "Took a lot for you to come here like this, after what I said, you know that?"

"No, I'm weak. It's just . . . my weakness got to where it was a foolishness I couldn't tolerate any longer." Her eyes glowed. "You'll be my strength now, Boone, so none of that matters."

"But it can't be, Chris," he said, tight-lipped with misery. "You know why. This dirty damn' frame-up. Chet Bannerman — his old man thinks —"

Her fingers on his lips silenced him. "Hush now. It will all come out somehow — I believe that." Her voice broke. "Oh Boone, it's got to."

CHAPTER SEVENTEEN

After leaving the hotel, Sam Ashby walked the two blocks to the Blackjack Bar — the cold decision in him not touched by the cottony heat that clung to the dusty street though the sun was far-westered, the shadows lengthening. The Spanish Spade men who'd lingered on the street had by now joined the others in the Blackjack. Nearing it, Sam caught the boisterous lift of voices, an explosion of laughter.

A lot of men to oppose his next move, he knew bleakly . . . and they would oppose it, given a moment to collect their senses. His best chance was a bold fast maneuver, then a quick retreat. Don't think about it, do it . . . while you're just mad enough to bring it off with a cool head, he told himself.

Sam paused by the row of saddle horses racked before the Blackjack, remembering something. Then he slid in next to Milo Squires' lineback dun, lifted Milo's rifle from the scabbard.

"Find something interesting?"

Without haste Sam swung his glance across the saloon doors, thrust ajar by Milo's squat and brutal form. His gibing words were slurred by whiskey, his broad face ruddied by it. Sam shoved the rifle into its sheath, ducked under the tie rail and stepped across the plankwalk, fronting Milo. "That old .50 Springfield of yours, maybe. I was checking for a one-shot rifle. You got one."

"So do a lot of men, Sammy. You want to make something of that?"

"Maybe."

"Better swallow the meal in your mouth, boy —"

At that moment Chip Suggs lurched out past Milo and faced Sam, with a glazed and bloodshot glare. His sad hound's face was convulsed with a purely drunken grief. "You killed Leo, deppity. You cut him clean in half. Leo was my frien' —"

He looped a long, awkward punch at Sam, missed as Sam stepped unhurriedly back. Suggs staggered off-balance. At once Sam, without warning, drove his left elbow savagely into Milo Squires's middle — then palmed out his Remington and whipped it up and down. Chip, solidly beefed by the arcing barrel, fell soddenly across the walk. Squires was still doubled up, wheezing with pain, when Sam rammed his gun against the foreman's ribs. He lifted Milo's gun from its holster and shoved it in his belt.

The balance of the crew had been moving forward toward the swingdoors in an ominous body, but the vicious and uncompromising abruptness of Sam's move brought them up short, as he'd guessed it would.

"Bill," Sam called to the bartender inside. "Set 'em up for every man. Pay you later on." His tone altered to flinty softness. "Want you boys to have a drink on me, each and every one of you. Meantime Milo and me are going to have a private talk. I won't take kindly to interruptions."

On the heel of his final word he grabbed Milo by the shoulder and flung him roughly off the walk for a half-dozen stumbling paces. Sam tramped after him, and something open and wicked in his face stopped Milo in his tracks as he wheeled around, a heavy fist lifted.

Without halting as he reached the foreman, Sam thrust a hard palm against his chest and sent him reeling away. Squires cursed bitterly, but didn't wait to be pushed again; he preceded Sam, matching his pace. "The hotel, Milo," Sam murmured. "Don't make me show you where it is."

As the two of them crossed the lobby, Sam said over his shoulder to the startled clerk, "Going to be a conference, Andy, up in my room. Apt to be noisy, but don't let it bother you. Don't let it bother anyone else either."

"What?"

"A conference. Just Milo and me. No outsiders, understand?"

"But damn it, Sam . . . !"

"You see to it, Andy."

They mounted the steep stairwell, Milo's stocky form slogging up ahead, his back stiff with rage. Sam halted in the murky hallway by his room, unlocked it without taking his eyes off Squires. He glanced briefly at Whit McKeogh's closed door at the far end of the hall, hoping that what ensued wouldn't disturb the injured sheriff. Sam motioned Milo into his room, swiftly bent to lay his own gun and Milo's on the hall floor, then followed Milo inside. He closed the door and locked it, pivoted on his heel to face Squires who stood with his feet apart and his thick fists closed.

"Just the two of us in a locked room — no guns." Sam tossed the key in his palm, pocketed it. "You can take that away from me, anytime you want to try."

Squires visibly relaxed, a bland amuse-

253

ment replacing his wariness. "Your wits still addled from all that booze a spell back?"

Sam suffocated his flaring wrath at the man's utter and unshakeable gall, saying thinly, "You know what I want. The truth. If I have to beat you half to death to get it."

Milo cocked a tawny sickle of eyebrow, grinning. "Got to get a bottle of what you been drinking. Makes a man think he's a gun inspector and I don't know what-all —"

"I make your gun the one that cut down on me out at Deaf Murchison's."

"Boy howdy, if you ain't a caution to snakes. You know that, why'n't I in jail? Where's your proof?"

"I'll have it. The whole dirty story. Before either of us leaves this room."

Squires sighed, shaking his head pityingly. "Fella, you gotten bigger'n your boots. Don't buck what you can't lick. Be smart, give me that key —"

"I told you how you can get it."

Milo laughed, the sound easy and confident, took a step forward with his hand held out. "Come on, let's have —" Abruptly his hand formed a fist, lashed viciously upward.

Sam, expecting the try, tilted his head and rolled back a step and the fist grazed along his jaw. He stepped in then and slugged

Milo in the face with a straight right, chopped his left fist against the base of Squires' bull neck, as if driving a nail. Then brought up the heel of his palm against Milo's chin and snapped his head back. Jarred to his toes by this hard fast punishment, Milo hit the floor in a sprawl. He scrambled to his hands and knees, came off the floor with teeth bared in a snarl and piled head-first into Sam who flung his crossed arms in front of his belly for protection. Even so, Milo's head bored relentlessly against his chest and carried them both into the wall with a smashing impact.

Squires pinned him there with his great leaning weight, his head buried in Sam's shoulder while he drove short pumping blows into the deputy's ribs. Sam gagged for breath, pummeled at Milo's ducked head with blows weak and lacking leverage, his knuckles glancing off the hard round skull.

Then he flexed his raised arms, with all his strength drove both elbows between Milo's massive shoulders and his hunched head, connecting painfully with his ears. Squires howled and plunged away as though seared with hot iron, his hands clapped to his head.

Sam saw nothing but Milo's contorted

face and he went doggedly after it, breath racking his sore lungs, and he hit out and connected. Milo's nose crunched and he went backward with his arms flailing for balance. Sam fired a looping overhand at Milo's chin but caught him in the throat, and Milo toppled across the bed. He kicked out blindly and caught Sam in the thigh and then he scrambled across the bed, hit the floor rolling and started to get up. Sam dived across the bed and caught Milo full in the chest with his hunched shoulder and the pair of them crashed to the floor.

For a moment they sprawled side by side, stunned, and then Sam got a knee beneath him, heaved to his feet and grabbed Milo's collar, dragging him partly upright. Milo dazedly tried to protect his face and Sam drove his elbow straight between Milo's hands and met the point of his jaw — felt the shock of it to his shoulder. Squires arched backward and his upper body crashed through the pane of the lower window sash. The sill caught him behind the hips, and the glass shattered by his back-plunging weight showered down on the tar-paper roof of the lean-to directly beneath. Hung half-in and half-out of the room, Milo thrashed his arms helplessly and then Sam reached through and yanked him in, flinging him against the floor.

Squires skidded on his side — something fell from his vest pocket and tinkled on the floor. Sam bent and picked it up. Turned the object in his hand for an uncomprehending moment before the icy shock of realization cut through his scarlet rage.

A little thing . . . a tarnished heart-shaped locket on a broken chain.

Milo Squires groaned deeply and rolled on his back. Lifted a bleeding face full of murderous hatred which vacantly dwindled as his gaze found the locket in Sam's hand. For the first time Sam saw fear, naked and crawling, stab out of the man.

"The locket," Sam panted. "Susie Wells's locket. It was you, Milo — you did that — raped and killed her, like you killed Paddy and my Nancy —"

"No," Milo wheezed. "You're crazy . . . Ashby . . . wasn't me . . . done any of that. . . ." Sam moved above him, a fist closing, and Milo shrank against the floor. "It was Chet, dammit!" he yelled. "Listen . . . it was Chet. I found it . . . in his jacket . . . the locket. I guessed he done it . . . so I looked for —"

"Or maybe," Sam cut in, "you took it off his body — after you killed him."

Milo Squires was in a trap. Sam saw the

furtive, miserable fear glide thinly beneath his sagging features, robbing them of sly blandness, numbing his thoughts past glib falsehood. He tried to struggle upright, and Sam promptly set his foot on the man's chest and drove him savagely against the floor. Milo gagged for breath. Sam let up his weight slightly, saying between his teeth, "I'll give you some wind, Milo. Enough to talk. Before you lie again, remember — this locket is enough in itself to hang you. So mister, tell it straight, every damn' word. If you lie, I'll know it. . . . You were riled enough that time I beat you to try for me. Only you shot my wife by mistake — then Delaney — didn't you?"

He applied a vicious pressure, and the admission left Milo in a pained bellow. "Yes, goddam you, yes!"

Sam took his foot away . . . put his shoulder against the wall and fought the crazed impulse that rocked his mind. Won over it, but found only an empty victory. Having the truth at last, he felt like a drained and hollow man. With an effort he pulled himself together. "Keep talking, Milo. Keep talking."

In broken, labored phrases Squires told how, seething with his single-minded hatred for the man who'd bested him in front of four others, he had fired in an instant, at the blanket-coated figure in the lamplit window . . . then had no choice but to kill Paddy Delaney when the deputy had tried to run him down. It wasn't till he'd cut out at a panicked gallop on hearing Sam call out, mistaking him for Delaney, that Milo had realized his first victim wasn't Sam.

A second cold fact had hammered home to him then. He'd counted on killing Ashby, and Ashby was still alive . . . which meant that he'd be on the trail of the killer. The law required solid evidence of guilt, but to escape Ashby's wrath he'd need a damned sound alibi.

None of the crew at Spanish Spade, all of whom had felt his ruthless bullying, would help him now . . . so Squires turned in blind flight toward Elkhorn. Thanks to the storm, no one had seen him ride in, and a few minutes' prowling outside the lighted windows had showed him Paco Morales alone in Stodmeier's saloon. It was a long chance he took next, a desperate notion born of a cornered man's panic. But he'd bluffed it through convincingly, first forcing Paco to alibi for him, then cowing the boy into a terrible oath.

The rest had gone much as Sam had guessed. While fairly certain that the enforced vow would seal Paco's lips for a long time, Milo had been left with a gnawing uncertainty. While not willing on that basis to brazen out another risky killing, he'd seen his golden opportunity to silence the Mexican for good when Paco Morales had become an abrupt scapegoat for rape and murder. But the lynching attempt Milo had instigated failed, and moreover he now had the terrified certainty that sooner or later, faced by the scaffold, Paco would definitely break down. Hence his attempt to shoot Paco in his cell.

When that had failed, Milo had spent a sleepless night full of jittery apprehensions . . . for Paco would certainly make a reasonable guess as to the identity of his attempted assassin — one more goad toward breaking of his oath. Milo had the strong impulse to pack his gear and slip quietly out of the basin without further ado. But he couldn't simply shed like a discarded garment his proudly held foremanship of a great ranch, a goal he'd slaved long hard years to achieve. Further, if he ran out knowing that Paco might have talked, he'd live afterward in the indecisive terror of a hunted man.

Milo made his decision. The next morning he had split off from the rest of the crew on-range, saying he meant to check the fence at Ten Mile Spring. Once out of sight, he rode fast and hard to Elkhorn. For the townfolk, it was still an ungodly early hour, and Milo grimly resolved that this time he'd succeed. Leaving his horse, he'd slipped up unseen alongside the courthouse, only to find the torn hole in the jail wall. Paco and Vicente had escaped.

A few minutes later, hidden where he could command a view of the entire street, Squires saw the sheriff and Sam leave the hotel and head for Celsa Gutierrez' shanty. He'd watched Sam and Celsa ride out together and then guessed accurately what was happening. It was a simple matter to follow the two at a safe distance clear to Deaf Murchison's, even cutting in a head-long circle to work ahead of them. Then, motivated by his blind hatred of Sam, he hadn't been able to resist setting up the ambush — the set up was ideal.

His crushing failure to bring it off, to get either Sam or Paco, had crystallized his mounting terror into his one remaining hope — flight. He'd need money to take him far and fast. And it hadn't taken him long to find the solution.

He'd guessed the truth about Susie Well's death the night it happened; the little fluff had long been baiting Chet whenever young Bannerman hit town, flirting and teasing, driving Chet half out of his mind. Bannerman's rotten-spoiled son had never been right in the head where females were concerned anyway. When Milo had returned to Spanish Spade that night after Susie was killed, he'd thought to examine Chet's horse in the corral, found it still warm and lathered from a long hard run. Chet had wasted no time in getting back to the sanctuary of the ranch.

Later, Milo heard about the locket taken from the dead girl, and last evening when Chet had left alone for Elkhorn, he'd crawled through the window of Chet's room and made a meticulous search, turning up the bauble under Chet's mattress. He then had the solution to his dilemma . . . blackmail money which Chet could get from his father simply by asking for it. Later when the crew was alseep, Milo had quietly left the bunkhouse and waited by the ranch road for Chet to return — leaping from the shadows and dragging the kid from his saddle. Showing him the locket, he made his threat.

Only Chet hadn't responded as expected. Later he'd learned why — young Bannerman was already nerve-shaken from his attack on the Powers girl. Chet had torn away from Milo, snatching out his gun. Chet's shot was a near-miss, and Milo, instinctively, desperately, had returned his fire — Chet fell without a sound. Milo had retreated on the run to a shed, swiftly shed his shirt and hat and boots, swung unnoticed behind the vanguard of punchers awakened by the shots and spilling confusedly out of the bunkhouse. Afterward he was the first to return to the bunkhouse, collecting his discarded garments on the way.

Again he'd sealed a temporary alibi for himself — and again he decided to hold tight and sweat it out. But now Milo Squires was finished, broken by the interminable nerve-strain he'd endured.

Quite suddenly Sam found that he could no longer stomach the sight of the man. He stepped around Milo, walked to the door and unlocked it.

At once Squires erupted from the floor and dove for the window. Sam came wheeling about as Milo's hurtling-lunge carried him through the broken, lower pane, his body slamming heavily onto the lean-to roof beyond. Sam rushed to the window as Milo scrambled down the roof and pitched over its eaves. The deputy heard the falling clatter of cordwood as Milo hit the askew woodpile beneath, jarring it to collapse.

Sam started to swing a leg over the sill to follow, changed his mind and loped to the door, swung it open and scooped up his Remington from the hallway floor. Back at the window he leaned far out just as Milo broke into sight, running up the alley between the hotel and the bank. Milo veered aside at the mouth of the alley as Sam shot. Sam saw him break stride, his burly trunk half-twisted on his hips by the slug's impact — and then he was past the corner of the bank and cut off from view again.

Sam flung about and raced from the room, down the hallway and stairs and across the lobby. Squires had time to reach his horse by the Blackjack, kick into a run toward South Jackson — had almost reached the railroad tracks by the time Sam burst onto the street.

Sam raised his gun . . . lowered it. Milo's bulky shape was reeling in the saddle as his wiry pinto streaked out across the darkening flats.

Aware of a biting pressure inside his left fist, Sam slowly opened it and looked down . . . the locket on its broken chain. Badly hurt, Milo wouldn't get far . . . time enough later to pick him up. A more urgent matter was at end. He held in his hand the evidence that would save three innocent men from hanging. Milo's story and the locket to back it, would end for them a nightmare of injustice.

CHAPTER EIGHTEEN

General Lucius Bannerman turned the trinket in his hand, musing aloud. "Squires was never an easy man to understand. Hard-working, competent, even-tempered — that was the man I believed I knew. Yet — his strength was his greatest pride, and it became his worst weakness — a bully-boy obsession such as I've seen in some Army non-coms. They had to be cock of the barracks, or they were nothing. Sooner or later Squires had to lick every new man on the crew. He'd go very cleverly about it, goading them for days if necessary to make them throw the first blow. I endured that idiosyncrasy because, except for that, his work was impeccable.

"And Squires always won — till you whipped him and did a proper job of it. For such a man, that was too much to bear. On the frontier, it seems, men's feelings lie very close to the surface . . . and it's a small step to a bushwhacking to wipe out a grudge. Only that went wrong, and from that point the man was caught in a chain of events he couldn't control. . . ."

The General sighed deeply and dropped the locket into Sam's hand. At the same time his eyes lifted, and Sam saw the grey defeat, the deadness of full acceptance, mirrored there. He had absorbed and fully self-admitted the truth about Chet. Even knowing as he did the necessity of what he'd done, Sam Ashby felt sick. Yet the General still held himself ramrod-straight, his face like iron and his quiet words even, these wholly unrevealing of how the man's life-moorings had been cruelly, cleanly severed.

All of them, Stodmeier, Burkhauser, Ma Jagger, Boone MacLaughlin and Christine, Celsa and Vicente and Sam, had gathered at Ma's cafe . . . except for Paco Morales who had gone home to his Rosa — a strangely subdued and humbly grateful Paco, his burden of fear lifted now, yet leaving its lifelong scar on his carefree nature.

The others had waited for Bannerman's return after Sam had given one of his crew the locket and dispatched him to fetch the rancher. They were all quiet, a little tense still, before the reaction of overwhelming relief set in. They talked then, ate the big meal Ma and the girls whipped up and answered the numerous questions of avidly curious townspeople. Long after twilight, Bannerman returned at last. They all listened soberly to Sam's explanation to the General. Bannerman's reaction, though expected, banished their last apprehensions.

The General looked now from one to the other, his manner curiously gentle, less cold and precise. "My apologies for the bad day I've given you all, and especially the ladies." He hesitated. "How is Whit McKeogh?"

"We looked in on him a while back," Ma Jagger offered. "The man's restin' good. Doc says Whit'll be palaverin' crazy philosophy for another twenty years."

"I'm glad of that," Bannerman said reverently, adding almost inaudibly, "There are times when a man finds his soul bearing as much as it can."

He touched his hat with a brusquely courteous gesture, turned on his heel and walked out. A minute later he and his crew paced their mounts past the broad outwash of window light and were lost to sight on the dark lower street.

Otto Stodmeier released a long, profound sigh. "That is all, and thank the Lord for it."

"Not all," grunted Abe Burkhauser. "You forgettin' Squires?"

Sam shook his head. "Milo's out in the basin somewhere tonight, no water or food, and hurt bad. He won't go far and I'll track him down tomorrow. Now I'm dog-tired, and I know the rest of you are. Let's call it a night."

Otto suggested, "You would maybe like a drink, Abe?"

"I'd like about a dozen," growled Burkhauser.

"To my place, then." The two old men tramped out, waving aside Sam's word of thanks.

Sam turned to Ma Jagger. "Owe you a vote of gratitude, too, Ma . . . and you, Celsa."

Ma snorted. "If that's all you got to say, I might's well say good night." She vanished into the kitchen, leaving both Sam and Celsa a little flushed.

Vincente Gutierrez looked from his sister to the deputy with puzzled eyes. He said tentatively, "You want me to walk home with you, hermana? If you got some hard words for me, I don't blame you none."

"What have I got to say to you?" Celsa demanded irritably. "Por Dios, how much longer you got to have someone standing by to wipe your nose?"

There was an awkward pause, then Sam put in, "There's that homestead of yours. If you're still serious about the idea, I'd suggest alfalfa. Reckon the local ranchers would be more'n agreeable to that kind of cropping, pay you handsome for whatever you can raise."

Vicente was silent a suspicious moment. "This comes from you?"

"Do I got to spell it out?"

Vicente's smile flashed in his dark face. "Gracias." He touched Celsa's arm, a quick, affectionate gesture, and walked out with his back straight, and quite proud.

Sam said then and sternly, "As for you, MacLaughlin, why not swallow that surly-bear pride sticking in your craw, go to Bannerman and ask him to open up that creek branch of yours he dammed off? Surprise me if he don't oblige you, now. That dried-up graze was choice once, could be again."

Boone MacLaughlin started to scowl, caught himself and glanced self-consciously at Christine. He cleared his throat, muttering that it might be a good idea.

Christine could not hide her radiant joy as she firmly took his arm, saying, "Take me home now, Boone. . . . Good night, Mr.

Ashby. Will you be very long, Celsa? Oh, there's so much I want to talk about — I won't be able to sleep until I do!"

Celsa smiled at the breathless outburst, nodded tolerantly. "I will be along soon, dear." When they had gone, she said with a resigned sigh, "She is so very young."

"Got all of three years less than you," Sam agreed soberly.

Celsa laughed softly, and it was a pleasant sound Sam hadn't heard. "You know what I mean. Celsa, always the brooding old mother hen." She picked a bit of lint from her skirt, not looking at him. "I have had enough of that, I guess."

"I think so, too."

She gave him a sidelong glance, her eyes very gentle and musing. "Still, it will be hard for them, Sam. They are very different, those two . . . will it work between them? Chris, she is so — so sensitivo, and he is so rough."

"Boone never had a chance to be much of anything else," Sam said quietly. "Where there's a big enough need — people can change."

"Yes."

They sat side by side on counter stools, and Sam studied her sharp, strong profile and saw more than beauty there. He still

felt a faint wonderment at the close understanding which had sprung between them
almost without words. He would never
forget another woman and what she had
given him, nor would she ever be dead to
him — not while memory remained warm
and undimmed. She had filled a part of his
life, and that part was over, and time and
life moved along a river that gathered to
itself new currents. You couldn't foresee all
its windings, but you moved serenely to its
bidding and kept your eyes forward. It
would be very different, the part that lay
ahead, for change was the great law. But it
can be good, Sam thought, It will be good.

"And so the greaser boys go free," Celsa
said suddenly, with a trace of acrid bitterness. "Some people will not like that."

"They'll get over it," Sam said grimly.

Celsa nodded and then said almost shyly,
"I will help Ma close up the place — and
maybe you take me home?"

"Reminds me that I haven't locked up the
office," Sam said, and swung off his stool,
heading for the door. He paused there and
turned. "I won't be long."

"If you are, maybe I won' wait," she said
tartly. But she smiled then, and so did Sam.

Walking toward the courthouse, he felt a
strong buoyancy, an uneasy excitement, like

a kid primed for his first buggy-ride with a girl. He shook his head at such foolishness but felt a curious tolerance toward it. He supposed that a little romantic falderal was all right in its place. . . .

He opened the door to the darkened sheriff's office, paused on the threshold to fumble out a match and strike it alight, preparatory to a cursory last check before he locked up. At once a strong draft guttered the flaring matchflame and it died. He softly swore, reached for another match — froze to the spot.

The draft had angled diagonally across the room . . . from the cellblock corridor. But he recalled quite distinctly that he'd tightly closed the heavy oak door that blocked it, after he'd released MacLaughlin and the two Mexicans. The cells held no other prisoners, so there'd been no visitors. Yet that door was partly open. . . .

The deadly significance flashed across his mind in the instant that he heard the slightly ajar oak panel creak to the thrust of a moving weight. Sam melted to the floor a second before the shot crashed deafeningly in the room's confinement. He scrambled wildly over to the desk, hugging its shelter as a second slug caromed off the top.

The strong draft caught the outer office

door and slammed it shut.

Now they were cut off from the street, its life and noise — Sam and his assailant — alone in a closed room. A drift of burned powder stung Sam's nostrils. His Remington whispered from leather and he crouched motionless, listening to an on-running silence — straining his ears for a betraying scrape of boot or whisper of clothing.

At last he said very softly: "Milo?"

A hollow chuckle. "Waitin' for you, Sammy. Come on ahead."

Milo Squires' voice was taunting — and weak. That was it, then . . . Milo had been too badly wounded to ride far, had known he'd stand small chance in the open against Sam and maybe a posse who'd come after him by daylight. He'd used his last strength to return to Elkhorn after darkness fell, had slipped up in back of and around the courthouse, let himself in by the unlocked sheriff's office. Had waited within the cellblock entrance, mastering his pain and weakness because he was willing to die on his feet if he could take the man he hated with him.

And he'd nearly succeeded . . . had Sam gotten a match fully lighted, giving Milo a solid target. The faint stiffening of Sam's silhouette in the doorway had betrayed Sam's recognition of a trap, and so he'd barely escaped Milo's first shot. . . .

Slowly now Sam's eyes filtered dim outlines out of the gloom. Faint moonlight streaming through the front window helped. He raised his eyes above desk-level and saw that the cellblock door, which swung into the office, had creaked fully open in that last gusty draft. The pitch-black rectangle of the doorway was plain . . . and unseen within it was Milo Squires.

Sam fired into the blackness. The slug screamed off an iron bar and ricochetted twice . . . Milo's unsteady, mocking laughter mingled with the clamor of tinny echoes.

"Try again, Sammy."

Squires was crouched out of Sam's angle of fire. Hugging the scarred old desk, Sam set his teeth against a crawl of panicked tension . . . shifted a cramped leg. His knee struck a tin bucket full of discarded wastepaper.

Sam considered a moment, his heart pounding. Then he felt inside the bucket, stirring the crumpled wads of paper. He laid his gun on his thighs, took out a match, struck it on the bucket rim and shielded the glow between cupped hands as he touched it to the paper. He shook the bucket to swiftly distribute the flames; a bright-leaping flare of orange wiped back the blackness.

Milo's nerve broke; his weak yell was drowned by the roaring blasts of his gun, and the shots were wild. Sam clamped long fingers around the bucket and heaved it overhead into the blackness of the corridor. It clashed loudly against a pair of cell bars and rebounded to the floor, scattering its flaming contents. His gun in hand, Sam sprinted across the room, toward the corridor now illumined by a fitful dance of light.

He had a chaotic and fleeting impression of Milo Squires stamping futilely at a burning wad, holding his thick body erect with his arm wrapped around a bar . . . but now seeing Sam; Milo did not hesitate. He fired before Sam could halt his veering run, the gun roaring a scant two yards away. The gunflash momentarily blinded Sam, even as with straining haste he tilted his Remington to bear, and he awkwardly fired as he lunged for the stone floor.

An instant later rolling on his side, he could see again. . . . Milo's great bulk washed into his spotty vision. That bulk was slipping downwards, its knees hinged and his gun dangling loosely in its hand — held upright still by the grip of a powerful arm around the bar. Then the shaggy head rolled limply on Milo's bull chest and the arm straightened and he fell.

The dying scattered-flames flicked their last as Sam, on his knees, felt for Milo's wrist, for his pulse — there was nothing, and then the light sank to smoldering sparks and Sam knelt in the darkness. Slowly he got a foot under him, rose, stumbled to the doorway, groped through and across the office and opened the outer door. . . .

She was standing in mid-street and she came to him, running the last few steps. She turned her head into his shoulder and stood trembling against him. Sam heard the sounds of a gathering crowd, but these meant nothing.

Celsa lifted her face. "Squires?"

"Dead . . . he was waiting. Maybe an hour or more."

"While we were just down the street —" She broke off and shuddered and then straightened, drawing back from him. "It is over then . . . *termino,* Sam."

"No," he said gently. "Just a time to forget. This is a beginning, Celsa."